The Woman Who Knew Gandhi

ALSO BY

KEITH HELLER

Snow on the Moon

Man's Loving Family

Man's Storm

Man's Illegal Life

The Woman Who Knew Gandhi

Keith Heller

A MARINER ORIGINAL
HOUGHTON MIFFLIN COMPANY
BOSTON • NEW YORK 2003

Copyright © 2003 by Keith Heller
ALL RIGHTS RESERVED

For information about permission to reproduce selections from this book, write to Permissions, Houghton Mifflin Company, 215 Park Avenue South, New York, New York 10003.

Visit our Web site: www.houghtonmifflinbooks.com.

Library of Congress Cataloging-in-Publication Data

Heller, Keith.
The woman who knew Gandhi : a novel / Keith Heller.
p. cm.
"A mariner original."
ISBN 0-618-33545-5
1. Gandhi, Mahatma, 1869–1948—Fiction. 2. Letter writing—Fiction. 3. Married women—Fiction.
4. Friendship—Fiction. 5. England—Fiction. I. Title.
PS3558.E47614W66 2003
813'.54—dc21 2003040609

Printed in the United States of America

Book design by Robert Overholtzer

MP 10 9 8 7 6 5 4 3 2 1

This novel is dedicated to
the memory of my father-in-law,
JAIME METER (1918–1999),
and my mother-in-law,
REBECA LISCHINSKY (1924–2002),
and their wonderful
fifty-one-year marriage.

I would like to thank the following people for their inestimable help: my agent, Irene Moore; my editor, Heidi Pitlor; my friend John Oxley of Hedge End; and Feroz Khan, the director of the play *Mahatma vs Gandhi,* in which he also acted the part of Harilal Gandhi.

The essence of being human is that one does not seek perfection, that one *is* sometimes willing to commit sins for the sake of loyalty, that one does not push asceticism to the point where it makes friendly intercourse impossible, and that one is prepared in the end to be defeated and broken up by life, which is the inevitable price of fastening one's love upon other human individuals. No doubt alcohol, tobacco and so forth are things that a saint must avoid, but sainthood is also a thing that human beings must avoid.

—George Orwell, "Reflections on Gandhi"

The Woman Who Knew Gandhi

I

As events turned out, it was a stroke of good fortune for Martha that her husband had never shown the slightest interest in the morning's post. Samuel wasn't much of a letter-reading, letter-writing man anyway. Bills, adverts, and flyers, the odd inquiries from friends and former customers wondering where he'd got to — these were the only pieces ever addressed to him. Most of the Houghton family was gone by now, except for a mad half brother still brooding about the perimeter of Imber after the army's forced evacuation of the village five years ago. As for writing, corresponding with the children and the grandchildren was Martha's work, not so much because of any preference in her or disinclination in her husband, but because of their handwriting. Samuel's was spidery and crabbed, even before the arthritis took hold, and helping with their two daughters' schoolwork at the kitchen table had always embarrassed him. Only with their son's Meccano Erector set in the shed out back had he felt at all secure. Martha, though, wrote like a medieval scribe, swirling her capitals into great gestures and trailing her sentences off into spirals that formed dark arabesques across the page. She took such lovely pains even over each week's grocery list.

Not like the unfamiliar hand on the blue envelope that she now separated from the rest, the only one today made out specifically to her, yet with no return address. She sat alone in a fall of rare February sunlight through the kitchen windows and let her tea grow cold as she studied the writing. In a child's block printing, as stiff as farmers in suits, the letters of her name and address jostled against one another, sometimes tripping over their neighbors' feet. The envelope itself seemed cheap and well traveled. Its corners were blunted, and the fabric of its paper was thinned by abrasion. But what had caught her attention from the first were the stamps. There were three different types, pasted haphazardly across the top as if in a feverish attempt to make up enough postage for the long journey. One was of a four-motored aircraft, another was of a waving flag, and the third was of a pillar crowned by carved lions. What they all had in common, in addition to some incomprehensible characters that looked like the hooks and eyes down a lady's dress, were the printed notices "15th Aug. 1947" and "India Postage." It was these legends, along with all the shifting colors of blues and grays, that had startled Martha at the letterbox and brought her pattering breathlessly back into the house.

She didn't open the envelope at once. In fact, she planned to do so only tomorrow, when Samuel would surely be out of the house, idling around the public green at the end of the street or, if the weather had turned foul, in the Fountain Inn pub in St. John's Road. Dr. Little had lately lectured him on the benefits of exercise. "You're not getting any younger, Samuel, and just because you don't have your ironmonger's any longer doesn't mean you should sit at home like some old woman." So Samuel had added to his usual mulling over newspapers and catalogs a regular constitutional that kept him out for half an hour or more. He never invited Martha, probably because the first time he asked her she'd told him she had better things to do than traipse about a village that she already knew better than she knew her own rugs. She hadn't, truth to tell, anything better to do, but it pleased her to fancy that some small part of each day still belonged to her alone.

Now, Martha thought as she glanced at the clock over the sink, to hide the letter before he returned. She sensed that it wouldn't do to tell Samuel about what she guessed must be a final communication from abroad. Not quite yet, at any rate, if ever. Besides, how could she ever make him or anyone else in Hedge End understand the mixed feelings that she herself had been struggling with for the past sixty years? The trouble was their home was small, even with the two floors, they had lived in it forever, and he had the craftsman's habit of reviewing his work whenever he passed it by. He would caress the grain of the bookshelves, lift the mattress to inspect the bedstead, and open and close the wardrobe doors to listen for crickets in the hinges. Always puttering, never satisfied with the tedium of retirement, he roamed the house from morning till night as though he had never left his old shop behind. She could never say where he might start rooting about next. Martha had even found him one morning deep in the cedar storage chest at the foot of their bed, handling the few silks and linens that the war had spared her as if he were a coal miner, trying to dig up his buried mates.

"What in the world — ?"

"I was only looking for the key to the lock on the back gate," he'd tried to explain. "It's gone missing."

"And you thought to find it in there?"

Samuel unconsciously removed a splinter from the lid of the chest. "I don't know. I've looked everywhere else."

The kitchen was perhaps the room he knew least well, so now Martha looked hurriedly around her. As she did, a surge of brighter sun illuminated the walls and cupboards, picking blinding glints out of every reflective surface. After considering and having second thoughts about the breadbox, tea cozy, and cutting boards, she hid the letter from India where she hoped Samuel would never look, under the covered bucket of rinds and crusts by the back door. Then, winded by her efforts, she stood for a while at the center of the room with her eyes half closed against the light.

Fifty-seven years earlier, the house back in Portsmouth had been Martha's only refuge. When her father had died of farmer's lung, her mother had turned to her unmarried sister for financial help. Aunt Feemy kept a boarding house for sailors in a street near Landport Terrace, a wry little structure of red brick walls and white window frames. As respectable as it could be so near a seaport, the house had welcomed Martha and her mother and put them to work at serving and washing and sewing. The young girl hadn't felt the move down from Droxford too sorely, though she did miss her blacksmith father and his comforting cindery smell. But in Portsmouth she had found compensations. The salty air blue, the burnished seamen's faces, and the drumming of boots across the dining room floorboards had all surrounded her with a noisy liveliness that reminded her of her father's workshop. If some of the other female lodgers were less honestly occupied than she and her mother were, and if some of the visiting men stayed for only an hour or so, Martha hardly noticed. She'd spent most of her time at an upstairs window, watching faceless passersby flicker like lighthouse beacons through the sea fog.

After Martha's mother died only a few months later, it seemed only natural for the girl to stay on at Aunt Feemy's. Her brother being away in the navy and her sister having already settled with her own family up at Avebury, Martha had nowhere else to go. Aunt Feemy was well read and curious, and she had insisted that the girl resume her schooling, at least informally, in the downstairs library. This was only a small room off the kitchen with three deal boards for a bookcase and a stool, with neither back nor arms, for a reading chair. The library consisted of fewer than twenty volumes: a history, two grammars, a geography, some unbound sheets of inspirational poetry, and the better novels of the local celebrity Dickens and the more distant Trollope. In this room, alone, Martha slowly grew into adulthood. Years of overheard conviviality, of artificial passions, in pages and in adjoining rooms, that were repeated often enough to become almost genuine, hadn't soured her at all. Rather, she counted herself lucky to experience at second hand what most women and men had to suffer at first. Knowing which of love's errors to avoid, she reasoned at the time, must be an invaluable lesson. It left her perfectly content to wait as long as she had to for the best and the wisest among men to show himself.

Until, that is, when she was sixteen years old, and the young man from India appeared. Having come to Portsmouth at the start of a cool and gleaming May for a meeting of the Vegetarian Federal Union in the Upper Albert Hall, he'd been brought to Aunt Feemy's by a fellow countryman. The newcomer to England was twenty-one, small for a man and dark, yet quieter and more intense than most of the other Indians who passed through the harbor. His ears were jugged boyishly out from the sides of his head beneath a smattering of oiled hair, and his eyes were more feminine and his lips fuller than any other man's that Martha had ever seen. Dressed as properly as a British gentleman in a dark morning coat, a starched Gladstonian collar, a white tie, and spats, he roamed wordlessly about the house, noting and seeming to judge everything, but commenting aloud upon nothing. His and Martha's paths crossed more than once that first day, on the stairway after the late breakfast or when they'd found themselves alone in the dining room. But then the girl was too slow to speak and the stranger too overwhelmed by the new world around him even to notice her.

It was not until that evening at the house's customary rubber of bridge when the young law student finally let down his guard. Aunt Feemy was in high spirits, even for her, leading the table in the kind of colorful banter that smoking and drinking and late nights so often gave rise to in her company. In a short time, Martha could see from her vantage point in the doorway that the two Indians were joining in with a fervor they seemed unaccustomed to, boys on bicycles they couldn't control. Spluttering and hiccuping with laughter, flushing burgundy above his striped silk shirt, the newest arrival had casually rested the back of his wrist against the arm of the hostess beside him. Aunt Feemy allowed the contact to linger and followed it with a meaningful stare, one that the flustered young man tried his best to return.

Toward the end of the evening, after he inexcusably fumbled a hand, he apologized at such length that Aunt Feemy finally became concerned.

"No, no, Mr. Gandhi, you play admirably enough, as if you've done so more than once," she reassured him. "Perhaps you're not the total innocent you would have us all believe."

"Still waters, Mrs. Keeve, still waters." The frightened face took on the approximation of a leer. "Even innocence, you know, sometimes requires testing."

He might have said or done more, but the other Indian — perhaps sorry that he hadn't intervened sooner — jumped in, "Whence this devil in you, my boy? Be off, quick!" And he pushed the student toward where Martha was standing and directed her to see the young fool up to his room. She did as she was told, eagerly preceding him up the dark staircase that had been the cause of more than one false step.

After turning on the gas sconce in his room, Martha made as if to scurry off to safety when the Indian begged her not to go.

"I feel such a fool," he'd whimpered, slumping down onto his bed. "Do you think your aunt will ever forgive me?"

"Aunt Feemy is the most understanding creature alive. You've no cause to worry."

"It's just that, you see," Gandhi continued, "my head's been all in a spin ever since I landed here. Everything is so different — so large, so loud, nothing like the soft, yellow dust floating in the air back home. And in order to complete my legal studies, I'm probably going to have to stay here in England for years!"

The young man had looked so forlorn that Martha sat down on the bed beside him, though with plenty of distance between them.

"I know exactly what you mean," she'd assured him. "I felt the same when I first moved down here from my hometown. And then when my mother died and left me here alone except for Auntie — well, I thought I'd never be able to go on. But I did, as you shall, too, I'm sure. It's always difficult, you know, starting something different, no matter what the personal circumstances might be. There are strange people and strange scenes, unfamiliar habits to get used to, and even daily changes in the weather that affect us more than we know. You just have to accept the fact that a new life is just that — new and whole. For a little while, you're going to be as helpless and as dizzy as a babe in a rocking cradle, but that will pass with time. It's not easy becoming someone other than who you were."

Gandhi smiled at her, and said, "You sound as if you know something about us Hindus."

"Not a jot." Martha smiled in return. "But I do know a little about being an orphan. And isn't that what you are now, Mr. Gandhi, though in your case by your own choice? Haven't you orphaned yourself from your home and your family? I can't imagine why you would, but —"

"To distinguish myself," he interrupted her. "Not as a famous man, but only as a man who might someday be distinguished from the endless crush of humanity. I should like to be a light, leading others onward toward goodness."

"Whereas I," she confessed, "can't think of anything more wonderful than a life lived among loved ones in peace and privacy. We shall have to keep in touch, Mr. Gandhi, and see which of us achieves his goal in the future."

Such a bold proposal silenced them both for a while, until the Indian added, "Tell me about your mother and your father and the rest of your family, could you? I'll tell you about mine."

And he did. Yet it was not until a year later, too late perhaps, that Martha had learned in a letter that the young man had a wife and an infant son waiting for him back home in India.

After nearly half a century of marriage, Martha could recognize her husband's way of opening a door even in a thunderstorm. Now the sound of the handle slipping and catching brought her back to the present, and she reached the front hall just in time to see Samuel fluttering a dust of snow off his coat. "Anything interesting come in the post?" he asked.

She pulled up short. "Today's? Why? Were you expecting something?"

"No letters or notices?"

She promised him that there had been nothing beyond the usual.

"That's it, then," he said, disappointed. "I suppose I shall just have to make do with the old motor catalogs. Still, you'd think that once a man's put in his request for the new ones . . ."

Relieved, Martha came forward to help him unknot his scarf and smelled the pub on his breath. His hands felt as cold as iron, and his face drooped with frustration. She offered to make him some cocoa. He could enjoy it right here on the sofa next to the fireplace. They could even listen to the Third Programme on the wireless together.

When, the following day, Martha finally came to open the letter, now wilted by the seeping of the rubbish, she was immediately taken aback by its signature, so different from the formal printing on the envelope. The writer was not, in fact, the former law student whose assassination at the end of last month had left her sitting motionless in a chair for hours. It was his eldest son, the same three-year-old boy he'd told her of in one of his first letters from India, only now he was sixty and dying slowly of tuberculosis somewhere in Bombay.

"My dear Mrs. Houghton," the letter read. "You will forgive me for pressing myself upon you like this with no preamble, but my late father always used to mention you as a friend whom I might turn to in any manner of distress. I find myself turning to you now at this sad moment, for I am woefully and fatally distressed."

Nonsense, thought Martha, fluffing out the sheet over her

cup of smoking tea. From what she'd learned over the years, her old friend and his first son had never got along all that well. There had been repeated betrayals on both sides, bitterness, regrets. It was unthinkable that the father should have confided in him anything about a relationship that, though never really shameful, had always been kept quiet by both of the principals involved.

"Lying here alone," the man continued, "I think I have come at last to a truer appreciation of my father and what he meant to the world at large. His passing is an incalculable loss to us all, but especially to me, estranged as we unfortunately were toward the end. Had I only known that murder would soon rob me of his wisdom and his compassion, I should have striven much harder to mend the breach between us before it was too late. Time, though, will have its way with us, will it not? And now, with my mother gone and the rest of my family scattered and busy with their own destinies, you, Mrs. Houghton, may be the last recourse available to me in my hour of trial. I only pray these words will reach you," a separate paragraph began. "I have no way of knowing how old is the address that I found among my father's papers. But what a strange sensation, to be speaking to someone who may never hear my voice! Much the same, I imagine, as when I commune every night with my father, in whatever exalted form he may now reside."

At the kitchen table, the daylight hiding phantoms in the muslin curtains that their daughter Alice had sent them last Christmas, Martha tried to picture the writer on the other side of the globe, just as she'd usually tried to picture Gandhi when he was away. But the distance was always too great for her to imagine anything clearly, even with the help of her friend's descriptions of his homeland and whatever newspaper and magazine photographs she could get her hands on.

Now, as before, Martha felt foreign and separate, isolated by time and space and condemned never to understand fully either the father or the son. Ever since the envelope arrived, she had been hoping that it might contain a last greeting for her, relayed through a third party perhaps, from the friend she hadn't heard from since the start of the year, a few final words that would have been blissfully unconscious of their own finality. But all she had were these before her.

Perhaps, she conceded, it was the son's illness that accounted for the letter's wandering tone, as well as for the drunken handwriting and the occasional familiarities. Martha had watched Aunt Feemy fade away from the same disease, the once rosy woman growing more and more transparent by the hour. And she shuddered to think of the same thing happening to her old friend's son, alone and afraid, writing from a deathbed to a woman he couldn't even know was still alive.

After some inconsequentials about Indian politics and the defeat of Hitler three years ago, the letter came abruptly to the point. "If you could only see your way clear," it pleaded with her, "to coming over for a short visit, here to Bombay, then perhaps I could return to you some of the memorabilia that I've collected since my father's death, and we two could reminisce about the man we both cared for so much. Ocean travel, I'm told, has resumed after the war, and you English must have plenty of money and leisure for such a voyage, more at any rate than have I. But, if you absolutely cannot come, could you tell me if your husband is still living and still with you at this same address? He would thank me, no doubt, for the opportunity to purchase the photographs now in my possession of you as a younger woman. They are quite fetching."

Martha turned the single page over, but found nothing

more after the signed name, "Harilal Gandhi." She shook her head as she stuffed the page back into the envelope. A common extortionist was all he was, hardly worth the sympathy she'd been feeling only a minute or two before. She pitied him his situation, as anyone would, condemned to a terrible death in a country that was now splintering dangerously apart under the weight of its newfound freedoms. But that certainly didn't give him the right to intrude upon her peaceful old age with all this nonsense about effects and photographs. Who did he think he was?

Still, on her way to finding a more secure niche for the letter upstairs, she decided that she might just write back to the dying man in Bombay. Only a note, distant and calm, enough to let him know that she had no intention of rushing around the world at his call. She would have to send it from nearby Botley, the Hedge End postmistress being notorious for her spying, but then Martha was used to taking such measures. At least Samuel needn't be put out by this unfortunate turn of events, and they could both return to their quiet, everyday lives. He'd been feeling so unwell of late in his lungs, and Dr. Little had privately cautioned Martha against upsetting him. The old man, he said, needed his rest.

2

MOST OF HEDGE END thought it a shame that Martha Houghton didn't act her age. On the far side of seventy, by all accounts, she could still be seen almost every day, running from shop to shop as if she were only half as old as she was. Granted, there was never any shortage in the village of energetic grandmothers in tweed skirts and woolen stockings, on foot or bicycles or even motorbikes, gossiping and nosing their way into every door and window between Upper Northam Road and Sunday Hill. But Martha Houghton was different. Unlike the others, she seemed less concerned with being seen doing something than she was with being, doing. She carried her own energy about with her as if it were a schoolgirl's sack, loaded down with joyful apples. Sometimes, on corners, she could be seen standing with her eyes closed and simply breathing, as if that act alone were intricate enough to be attended to in isolation. Then she would nod once or twice to herself and set off again, seeing to the chores that she didn't dare trust to the husband she loved in spite of his fondness for procrastination.

In appearance, especially in the eyes of her fellow villagers, Martha looked exceptionally solid and in good health, even after the rigors of the war's rationing. Her years had grayed her through and through, but they hadn't yet reached her heart, and she had as much time to spare for fallen toddlers as she did for herself. Jowly and very pale, she still seemed to have too many bones for such a small body. Yet, in motion or when she was simply using her hands, she assumed the animation of a teenager and danced in place for no reason. Her voice set her example. It was harsh and scraping, more of a drunken man's voice or the voice of the sea on the strand, and it left others precious little room for disputing or for even being heard. But in the St. John's Church choir, somehow, it always managed to blend in seamlessly with the rest of the congregation and mellow into song.

If anyone had anything to say against Martha Houghton, it usually had to do with her independent character. She was altogether too strong for Hedge End. Everyone knew her story. Raised in "that house" in Portsmouth, an orphan in most respects, she had finally become a teacher, and all under her own steam. First in Portsea, then in Southampton, and later in Botley in the school opposite All Saints Church, she'd gathered children about her as if in the folds of her skirts. According to the rumor mill of Mrs. Theaves, a dressmaker on the easternmost border of Hedge End, it was in this last position that the young woman had met one Samuel Houghton, then working in his family's carpentry shop near the Brunswick Dyers and Cleaners agent in Winchester Street. The man had been instantly impressed by the range of Martha's knowledge. Oh, she had always been quite booksy! Even Joyce and Lawrence had held few terrors for her. Nor had a brief flirtation with the suffragettes, inspired by the local example of the trousered Mrs. Valois, proved enough to frighten away the carpenter. He valued Martha most for her steadiness. She was, he often said, the only soul he'd ever known — male or female — who honestly didn't worry about dying. All that mattered to her was to continue, and that was all any man could ever ask of a lifelong companion.

Since moving to Hedge End directly after their marriage, the Houghtons had become a fixture on the north side of the village, not far from the strawberry fields. Their house was a narrow affair of rusty bricks, almost identical to those of their neighbors, with the same small patch of lawn in front and a longer swath in the rear with a squat shed for tools against the privet hedge. Samuel soon opened an iron shop in Bursledon Road, while Martha started working at the National School just down the street. This activity she pursued even after the three children came and went. "What more can I teach them," she asked anyone who would listen, "than that life is a series of lessons?" During the Great War, with Samuel gone to mind the machinery in Flanders, Martha had volunteered to serve at the rolling mills and had even taken her firstborn, Alice, with her. In the late war, too, both Martha and Samuel had marched out to the Empress Dock in Southampton to help the Yanks with their Fourteenth Port preparations for D day. Even with the blitzed warehouses rocking all around them, Samuel had supervised the building of floating cranes by the Caswell Company and, after the invasion, ferried military stevedores in civilian coaches. Martha had lent a hand at the port's Postal Regulating Station and with the temporary quartering of troops. The end of the war had simply seen them return to their calm, daily routines of household duties and the care of each other, both of them retired from working in name only.

Now their children were elsewhere, two with grown children of their own. Paul was a barber in nearby Northam, quiet and content with his lovely son and daughter, though his wife's nerves often kept their family teetering on a knife's edge. Nellie was more brittle and restless, a salesman's "widow," forever fretting over her house in Southsea with its patterned garden and sacrosanct fabrics. Nellie's older son, Henry, had been lost early in 1945 in the Ardennes, but since then, perhaps significantly, her regard for the proprieties had never flagged. And the first child, Alice, an unmarried teacher in Chichester, was independent and hard to please, somewhat cynical, but remained kinder and wiser than her parents had ever been. The home in Hedge End was finally cleared of all the roughhouse games and hourly crises of children growing, yet the Houghtons still seemed never to have done with their endless doing, Samuel with his motors and Martha with her reading and her needlework. Their lives hadn't been entirely free of tragedies, a son named Walter having died in their arms forty years ago of pneumonia as they tried to warm him before the open oven. But, through it all, Martha and Samuel had pushed on, and by now Hedge End took a reluctant pride in watching them trundle tirelessly around the village, either separately or together, as if they were gliding along on hidden rails.

Today, Martha had been noticed everywhere, even though the February sky was gunmetal in color and the air cold and sharp. Price Hindes, the greengrocer, had seen her getting off the bus from Botley and had marked the way she'd held a hand splayed across her breast as if to catch her breath. Mr. Patten had reported to his neighbor that he'd glimpsed her hat rounding the corner of his cheese shop and heading into the wind toward the church. And Mrs. Ladbrook, of no fixed profession, had sworn to no one in particular that Martha had come out of the Fountain Inn pub, alone and at midday, wiping the froth of a Marstons Burton ale off her mouth. By late afternoon, the old teacher had apparently scoured the area, as if she were searching for the solution to some new and vexing mathematics exam. But, as usual, her last and longest visit was to the Olympia, Rebecca Pye's combination bookshop, lending library, and loitering stall, Hedge End's mid-twentieth-century version of a village well without the well.

Rebecca had lost a husband to each of the world wars and was now married to a man half her age who protected himself by staying as far away from her boundless vitality as the dimensions of the bookshop and the house behind it allowed. Born and raised in Kansas, she had followed her favorite, T. S. Eliot, over to England, Anglicized herself, and opened a bookshop in the hope of someday having him in to sign copies, a dream that had yet to materialize. With a Midwesterner's hard-nosed practicality, Rebecca sold literature by the ounce and nonfiction by the pound, reserving her own passions for the Eastern philosophies that stood in such sharp contrast to the flat wheat fields, drawls of tobacco juice, and deserted Saturday-night diners of her youth. Calicoed and rodentlike, she sported more pins stuck in less hair than any other woman around and a gnawing expression about the chin that frightened businessmen and made all the girls giggle.

She was alone in the shop when Martha entered. Rebecca smiled broadly at the sight of her friend and walked with an outstretched arm toward a pyramid display of books and pamphlets that stood near the freestanding gas heater.

"What do you think? I do so hope that you, of all people in Hedge End, approve."

"This is all for him?" asked Martha as she came up to the carefully balanced stack.

"And why not?"

"But how long has it been here?"

"Why, a week or more!" cried the shopkeeper. "Don't you remember from your last visit?"

"Was I in?"

Martha began handling the top volumes as if she were examining fine silks, turning them over and over to judge their textures, inhaling the aromas of dust, sandalwood, and cedar sachets that created such a tranquil air in the cramped room.

"There are some new ones here," Rebecca encouraged her. "Some even you might not know of."

"Have this . . . had this and lost it . . . have this," murmured Martha, whose coat was now shining with melted frost. "What?" she exclaimed. "This here so soon? But I read of it only toward the end of last year."

They handed back and forth a book entitled *Satyagraha* and fingered its thick, dusky pages in respectful silence.

"That's a bit slow going, though," Rebecca commented at last. "I'd recommend instead Annie Besant's Theosophical work on Indian freedom or Rolland's recollections —"

"No, I've owned that one for years."

"Or," Rebecca went on brightly, hefting a pair of new books, "either of these memoirs, Millie Polak's about his time in Johannesburg or Muriel Lester's about the East End. They're both very good reads."

Martha Houghton stiffened and curled her nose. "I don't know." She sighed. "I've always thought it in such poor taste for someone to entertain a famous friend and then straightaway scamper off to write it up for public consumption. One oughtn't to gossip anyway, but if you're crude enough to take the whole world into your confidence, then how can you ever be trusted again? The entire relationship becomes a lie," she added. "And wasn't the truth the most important thing in life to him?

"But, hello!" she said with a start, groaning down toward the floor. "Here's something different. What is it?"

The other squinted and said, "Yes, that's a collection of his writings for his *Young India* journal, dating from the mid-twenties, I think. I haven't read them all myself yet, but toward the end there's a spirited debate about whether or not rabid dogs should be killed. Personally," Rebecca went on with a critical frown, "I think the master must have been ill when he wrote in defense of it, or his fasting had made him delirious. If not, how could he have ever advocated murdering animals that had never done anyone any harm?"

"Except to bite children and old women to death," Martha reminded her.

"Still," Rebecca insisted, "we either practice nonviolence or we practice violence. There can be no middle stand. And if Gandhiji didn't uphold *ahimsa* in every part of his life and death, then what's to become of the rest of us who lack his *mahatma,* his great soul? We might just as well have all perished along with him."

Rebecca, much to Martha's distaste, often indulged in the external trappings and jargon of the various creeds she followed. Yet this time her words served only to underline the recent loss of the man for whom the display had been erected.

"How are you getting on, Rebecca?" Martha asked in a more kindly manner. "Has any of the shock of it worn off for you yet? I know for myself it hasn't. I first heard the news on the wireless when I was sitting alone and knitting. I thought they said 'emancipation' instead of 'assassination.'

When I finally understood, I felt all my limbs go numb at once. It still comes over me the odd times, a feeling of being not quite connected to the world around me anymore, now that he's lost to us."

"How could anyone not feel that way?" Rebecca retreated toward her counter, adjusting hairpins as she went and finally inviting Martha to sit across from her. The bell on the top of the street door rang and they both turned, but it was only the evening wind. "I mean to say," she resumed, "the unutterable tragedy of it all. To have fallen a mere six months after having won what he'd worked his whole life for. And, especially, to the same kind of sectarian hatred that he'd always preached so desperately against. It's too much, Martha, don't you think? Isn't it simply too much for the rest of us to bear?

"Sometimes" — she pointed to her chest, as gaunt as a cuttlebone — "I feel such a pain in here that I think there may be a hole in one of my lungs, but Dr. Little says not. You know, the way it feels when you've a cough or when you've just woken up from the ether. I tell you, it's almost as if I've lost another husband, and that without ever having met the man face to face. I only hope they execute this Godse monster who killed him as slowly and as horribly as possible."

"*Ahimsa,* Rebecca," Martha whispered to her friend.

"What? Oh, all right, if you say so."

To console herself, the proprietress set a miniature pot on top of a spirit lamp behind the counter and brewed some blossom tea that she'd received from a correspondent in Assam. For being such a dedicated "Quit India" campaigner, Rebecca relied upon a surprisingly large network of colonial contacts and suppliers, most of whom had made their fortunes under the empire. But different times, she argued, created different contexts, a sentiment that she was sure her hero had understood better than any of them.

"It must be that way even now," she observed as she poured. "He hasn't really died, you see, only changed, only turned his head off to one side to view things from a slightly different perspective. It's we who have been left here, wondering how to fill his place with the sorry fools we have to work with. Have you read any of the articles and letters in the newspapers since his death?" she asked. "They're abominable. Very watery in their sorrow, most of them too, too neutral, and some even with a secret 'no-more-than-we-expected' smirk behind them that's ghastly. I've heard people in this same village — I could name names! — who have said in so many words that the master got no more or less than he deserved. How people like that can still have the face to call themselves Christians is more than I'll ever understand."

Rebecca shuddered and stole a glance at the window, as if she feared reprisals from her neighbors. But outside there was only pewter darkness and the first stirrings of snow and two or three stray motorcars, churning toward shelter.

"And then when I consider," she went on in a hush of awe, "how blessed you were, Martha, to have known him, to have actually been in his presence. Didn't you tell me once — in the strictest confidence, I know — that you and he had talked some down in Portsmouth during your girlhood there? How I envy you! Tell me," she begged wildly, a crumb of cream cracker adhering to her mottled lips. "Only tell me a little more about what he was like, and then I'll leave you forever in peace. I promise."

"Well," Martha began, "he was a man —"

"A godly man!"

"No." Martha smiled patiently. "Only a man. What I remember best about him are the small details — how excited he was to be someplace new, how serious he was about his studies, how he yearned for perfection in all things. He was hardly more than a boy then, and I'm sure a lot of things changed in him as the years came on, the same as in the rest of us." Martha paused and looked at a small enamel portrait of a blue god that was hanging on the back wall. "He was sleek and dark, but with a smile that could find you on the far side of a room, even when it wasn't meant only for you. Goodness was what you sensed in him at once, goodness and determination, or perhaps that was merely the impression he made on a young and silly girl."

Rebecca was wagging her head from side to side in a show of jealous admiration.

"Incredible! But the two of you never kept in touch after that one encounter?"

"What do you think?" Martha responded with an uncomfortable shift in her chair. "That a common schoolteacher should have the time and money to travel all the way to India at a moment's notice?"

"By post, then."

"With the mistresses we've had in charge of our office?" scoffed Martha. "The whole of Hedge End would have known of it before I'd reached my door. Besides," she reminded her, "you know very well that I met my Samuel only a few years after. And, once we were together, I'd never have dreamt of compromising myself with any other. Not that I didn't think about the company and the conversation that I remembered from Portsmouth. I did, more than once, and I still do, even after all this time. But what other choice did I have?" A sour look came over Martha's face, and she finished, "Don't forget, Gandhi was already married and had a son and a houseful of his own people back home. Surely no one could have expected him to throw them all up on a whim and stay on here indefinitely where he didn't even belong. Not just for me."

"It's strange, though," Rebecca persisted with a glance at the front window, now shining with frost, "that you never thought to meet up with him during any of his subsequent visits. Wasn't he in London time and again, twice or more before the Great War and once just at its start, and later even down in Chichester, where your Alice had gone? I know I always meant to go and try to watch him somewhere myself, but there were always those husbands of mine and their many illnesses for me to tend to. Now if I'd been you, I think I would have."

"You would have what?" Martha reached for more jam and tea. "Run panting after him like that Shelton girl in Ventnor or that Madeleine Slade who made such a spectacle of herself during the Round Table Conference in thirty-one? Don't you remember?" she asked, and the hairpins across from her nodded in grave disapproval. "The way the press said she slaved for him, kissing his feet and rubbing the English cold out of them and cleaning and washing for him and feeding him and even drawing his bath. But that wasn't the man I knew. The man I knew had a sight too much fairness in him to let any real friend of his lower herself so. Unless his fame had made someone else of him entirely, and that I simply can't and won't believe."

She fell silent, bothering a fragment of cracker across the counter until it tumbled off and down to the warped linoleum at her feet. She was so distracted that she didn't even apologize. And, even though she felt as if she were betraying their friendship, Martha said nothing to Rebecca about the letter she'd just received from India. All these matters were still too unsettled, still too private. "The worst thing," she said mournfully, "is that all the world knew of him, and yet so few truly knew him for what he really was. Me, I was too simple and childish to make much of the brief opportunity I had. And now it's too late, isn't it, even with all the words and pictures of him that are left us. It's just too late."

No one in Hedge End noticed Martha Houghton walking home that night. Another snow had started in earnest, and the low, full clouds had caught in the tight stands of trees and bent their branches downward. In weather like this, even the warmest windows in the village seemed to her far-off and unfamiliar.

The next day, housebound by the blizzard, Samuel treated the letter from India that Martha had finally turned over to him as if it were wholly beneath his contempt.

"I appreciate your honesty, dear, in showing it to me, but he's cracked, isn't he? Must be the consumption that's done it. Or he only wants money."

"I expect he came by our address from my subscriptions to some of Rebecca Pye's journals, his father's *Young India,* perhaps," Martha suggested. "Though I can't imagine what photographs he could be talking of."

"I shouldn't think you would," declared Samuel from the depths of his favorite chair. "Because he hasn't any! Or, if he has, they're only some casual quay photos that you don't even remember having been taken. You're not seriously letting this rotter bother you, are you, Martha?"

"I did write him back, I'm afraid."

Samuel sat forward with the Bombay letter drooping in his hands. His retirement had deflated him somewhat, and now the man who used to thunder rods and hammers about in his shop peered from behind thick eyeglasses, used a cane, and had a complexion the color of weak tea with milk. His knees were as sharp as his shoulders, and his shoulders were as sharp as a bird's, while his voice was sometimes too feeble for even his wife to make out.

"You didn't!" he cried. "But whatever did you say to him?"

"Only that I was sad for his condition and for his father's death and wished him the best, but that there was nothing I could do to help." On the other side of the spitting fire, Martha sat with an unread newspaper on her lap. "And I told him that my husband was alive and well," she said with a nod at Samuel, "and that neither of us had the least objection to his sending us whatever items he could spare. Though, having nothing to hide or fear from each other, we thought it beastly of him even to insinuate that we might, and he'd do better to save himself the unnecessary postage and use it for himself.

"I put that last bit in," Martha pointed out, "to keep him from pestering us again. We certainly wouldn't want him to start burying us beneath an avalanche of worthless mementos that mean nothing to anyone over here. They might bring in some little money from collectors, but I don't think we've come so low that we'd ever want to gain from another man's death. Would we?"

"Wise of you, Martha, wise," agreed Samuel, though he seemed disappointed, after all, that the adventure should have come to nothing so soon. "No," he went on with a quizzical look, "we certainly wouldn't want that. But I'm sure the fellow hasn't got what all to trade with anyway. How much mischief could the pair of you have done? Walk the streets? Visit the harbor? It was only a passing fancy, right, between a couple of youngsters?"

Again, he sounded ever so slightly let down, as if even the most indirect contact with such a famous world figure might have added a borrowed luster to his life.

In answer, Martha at first demurred, but then she reviewed once more the blameless circumstances of her meeting with the Indian law student. She made it clear that her husband had no reason to feel any resentment or suspicion and that no one else knew of the encounter. She was only happy to find that he wasn't troubled to learn that the Aunt Feemy she'd been telling him about for years had run a house of uncertain virtue. All the rest, she maintained, was nonsense, so much so that she hadn't even thought it important enough to recall — before now.

"You've never doubted me, have you?" she asked him. "I should hate to think you had and didn't tell me. And all this was so long ago!"

Samuel replied, "Yes, it is rather late in the day now for any of that. What's either of us going to do at our age?" he said and forced a laugh. "Sue for divorce and find ourselves new loves?"

"Samuel!" Martha tossed the newspaper into the fire, where the pages writhed into ash. Then she rose to her feet and walked toward the stairs, her gait a fraction less steady than usual. She said she had a basket of sewing to attend to.

"This Gandhi, though," her husband remarked as she passed, "even as a young man must have had no end of interesting tales to tell. Coming all the way from India as he did."

"Oh, yes, we just talked and talked and talked," she said over her shoulder. "But really about nothing in particular."

"Just talked?" Samuel called up after her.

But Martha was already too far upstairs to hear him, and he was left alone with the letter from the dying stranger in his hands.

3

ONCE A WEEK, usually on Thursdays or Fridays, Martha took the bus into Southampton to visit her son and his family. As a rule, Samuel stayed at home, not so much because he'd given up driving long ago as because the riding made him dizzy. During the last war, when the city had groaned with shelling and military activity, Paul's two children had fled with their mother to their grandparents' house while their father, whose lungs were as frail as Samuel's, had worked at recruiting. It had been an oddly happy time for the Houghtons, Martha and Samuel returning nightly to a front parlor filled with half-finished puzzles and forts built of rearranged furniture. For the first time in years, they felt as if they were beginning anew, as if time had relented and let them experience childhood all over again. Perhaps that was the true reason Samuel normally declined to accompany his wife on her weekly visits. He simply couldn't bear the awful weight of the nostalgia that came with them.

Martha herself suffered from some of the same. The ride

into the city wasn't a long one, but it still gave her enough time to reflect on the harrowing finality of growing old. "Better than the alternative," Samuel had often told her, but that hardly made up for all the stubborn regrets and thrilling changes that would never come again. Although she would seldom admit to being in any way dissatisfied with her life, Martha found outside the bus window plenty of sights that gave rise to wistfulness. Southampton had suffered greatly during the war, but in the last three years it had caught its breath and begun to stand erect again. And it was precisely this renewal that Martha responded to as the various neighborhoods passed her by. She saw bonnets in limping baby carriages that might have once belonged to any of her own children, and in the rattle of bricks into dustbins she heard the chuckling of tricycles down uneven walks. Successive versions of herself seemed to appear and disappear along the road, and she relished every moment of the passing review, despite what either Gandhi or Samuel would say to her if they were here.

This, she remembered, was what the student from India had found most exasperating about the young English girl in the Portsmouth boarding house. Even during the earliest hours of their acquaintance, a clear distinction was established between Gandhi's spirituality and Martha's worldliness that would only grow and intensify the longer they talked.

"But I've already explained to you," he'd said to her from his perch on her windowsill, "how the human soul has to struggle through countless lives until it finally reaches a state of ultimate, blissful rest. What the Buddhists call *nirvana,* we Hindus call *moksha* or *mukti.* It's the final release from the tiresome round of births and deaths and rebirths that must go on forever, if a man should fail to act right."

"Still," Martha had questioned him, "why would anyone not want as many lives as possible? Wouldn't that just mean more loves and more joys, more children, more memories —"

"And more suffering —"

"And more healing!" she had cried out with a stamp of her foot. But Gandhi had been unable to understand her objections in their first short afternoon together. Only now, perhaps, was he somewhere learning the vast difference between their separate points of view.

Paul's home and shop were situated in a quiet corner of Northam near the banks of the Itchen River. Beneath a stretch of elevated roadway stood a divided dwelling, the right half given over to a private home and the left to an aluminum door and a window of pebbled glass. Inside sat a trio of barber's chairs on a floor of white tiles and between facing strips of mirrors. Bottles of colored and perfumed water with metal spouts glowed from the sideboards, while from black cabinets leaked the friendly humidity of baking towels. The back door was always left open, no matter what the weather, so that one could see the smaller streets, wet with rain or sun, that clambered down toward the river. In this way, the interior shone like the steel cylinder of a telescope that gave a peek into secret alcoves rustling with elms and embroidered curtains.

Today, as always, Martha smiled at the card in the window that listed the shop's "Attempted Hours" as she entered to find her son lathering the cheeks of a man in a waistcoat and a suit.

"Mother! You're early. I'll be done here directly. Why don't you go next door?" Paul pointed with his razor at the wall. "Dorothy and the children are waiting for you."

"I think I'll just sit for a while," she said, backing toward a sofa. "But don't you hurry."

"Father didn't —"

"No, Paul. Not this time."

The man in the chair tensed at the barber's voice. There had never been any harsh words exchanged between Samuel Houghton and his only son over his choice of profession, but everyone in Hedge End knew the old ironmonger had felt let down. Perhaps if he himself had loved the heft of iron less, or if his son hadn't valued peaceful conversations over scissors quite so highly, the Houghton family business might have had a future. But, as it was, the shop in Bursledon Road had been sold to a vacationing Brummie who had immediately converted it into an emporium selling sinks, fixtures for bathing, and fishing lures. Even now, Samuel couldn't bring himself to walk down the shop's side of the street during business hours.

Paul Houghton was a tall man of thirty-eight, a final surprise for his parents to take the place of the first son who had died the year before. He had his mother's skeletal angularity and his father's sunken torso. During work, he wore a pale blue smock over an ironed shirt and a knotted tie and moved gracefully from counter to chair in a relaxed dance, never hurried, never unsure. A few of his neighbors may have found his good cheer maddeningly optimistic, even after the war's victory, yet they wouldn't have thought of patronizing any other shop. They prized him for his soft voice and attentive ears and for the way he had of making them all feel like boys again, and innocent.

His wife, Dorothy, was an excessively thin woman and a worrier whose unspecified anxieties manifested themselves as rashes on her arms, a racing heart, and a laugh that splintered like cracked glass. When she finally welcomed her mother-in-law into her home today, she fussed over her until Martha grew more concerned for the younger housewife than she was for herself.

"No, sit yourself down, dear, please," Martha begged as Dorothy tried to carry away her overcoat and plump up a chair at the same time. "Am I to understand that both the children are at home? But what about their school? I hope you didn't keep them out only for my sake."

"And why shouldn't we have?" Dorothy said shrilly.

"It's their school's buildings," Paul interposed as he hung up his smock. "There are still a lot of repairs to be made before they're perfectly safe. Toward the end, the Germans dropped a bomb no more than a street away. Now the children get one or two days of every week off, and oddly enough they don't seem to mind."

Martha peered from side to side in the narrow sitting room. "So where are my darlings?"

"Out in back. Making up your bed. Go on ahead, Mother," Paul said, motioning to her. "I'll lend Dorothy a hand with the dinner."

Martha never liked to be away from home for too long, especially at night, when Samuel's breathing kept him up and roaming about the house. But her stamina wasn't what it once was, and sometimes the ride back was more than she could manage at a late hour. On such evenings, after calling Hedge End to notify her husband, she stayed over in the grandchildren's room and shared their nighttime riddles and games. It gave her yet another chance to relive an earlier period of her life that was threatening to fade from memory.

They were there waiting for her now, having devoted their free day to decorating her bed with paper festoons, in case she decided to spend the night.

"Do you like it?" the girl asked with a saleswoman's wave at the display.

"Oh, I do, indeed."

"It took me absolutely hours to finish!"

Her brother pouted up at her. "What about me? Didn't I help?"

The girl ignored him and set about clearing a space on the littered bed for her grandmother. Tetty, at eleven, had already substituted for the natural wisdom of childhood the artificial knowingness of adolescence. She was impatient and grumpy, at least with her parents and her brother, and always talked in a louder tone than her voice could bear. Curves of baby fat still clung to her in awkward places, while her cream-colored Alice hairband and homemade dress seemed to shrink her in perspective. Whereas she had evidently been designed by herself and her mother, Malcolm was more a chance, working medley of elbows and knees, a nine-year-old flurry that carried, as his father liked to tease, no small amount of acreage underneath his nails. Both children were supremely good at heart, though the boy had perhaps less consciousness of it than his sister and was, therefore, only that much purer.

"Mother says you're not to go back until tomorrow," Tetty said to Martha. "She says the weather's worsening and at your age you need your rest and Grandfather shall have to do for himself as he should have learned to ages ago. She says," the girl added hurriedly.

"Perhaps she's right." Martha smiled. "Coming all the way into the city did leave me feeling a bit puffed out."

"Did you bring us anything?" Malcolm wondered after a suitable pause for consolation.

"Animal!" cried his sister.

"No, no, don't chide him. He's right. What sort of a granny should I be if I came to see my two favorites empty-handed?"

Scrabbling dramatically through her handbag, Martha emerged at last with, for Tetty, a miniature statue that was half human and half elephant and, for the boy, a small package of incense that she made him promise not to burn indoors.

"But even outside," she told Malcolm, "the odors are supposed to purify the air and bring you good fortune. It's the same with this." She reached out and stroked the seated bronze figure with the elephant's head. "His name is Ganesha, and he's meant to bring you, Tetty, all the wisdom and success you deserve."

"Where's his other tooth?" the girl asked, fingering the stub.

"He broke it off himself and threw it at the moon for laughing at him."

Tetty peered down at her brother, as if she'd always suspected him, too, of such supernatural mischief.

"You needn't pray to him or anything like that," Martha cautioned her, knowing her mother's church gloom all too well. "But I thought he might look fine on your bureau or even on a cord hung about your neck. Or we might put him together in September with some of your other dolls and make up what's called a Navaratri festival, where you set up platforms and a pavilion for your best playthings right here in the house. For some reason," she said in a falling cadence, "I've been thinking about such things lately, but I couldn't recall if I'd ever mentioned any of them to you before.

"Both of these, by the way, are from Rebecca Pye's shop," Martha went on as she prepared to make herself at home in the chaos of the bedroom. "You remember her, don't you, children? The little woman with all the books and the hairs like wires?"

"Oh, I do!" exclaimed Malcolm. "She's wizard!"

"You're so blindingly daft." Tetty shook her head in despair over her brother and moved off to commune privately with her new snaking curio of trunk and tusk.

For the rest of the evening, Martha divided her time between the adults in the sitting room and the children in the rear of the house. In most respects, she much preferred the latter. As deeply as she adored her only son, and as indebted as she was to him for certain favors, the company of his wife often proved unendurable. Never very strong, plagued since birth by twitches and quicksilver moods, Dorothy had been demolished by the war as visibly as any building. Even in the comparative shelter of Hedge End, she had developed hair loss and blind spots that had baffled Dr. Little. She had also claimed to be able to feel her internal organs detaching themselves, and the sweep of a brush or comb, she thought, stuttered directly over the corrugated surface of her brain. Many of these fantasies had survived in paler versions to the present day, until Dorothy had been forced to give over her work at a local dress shop. Now she let it be known that she would sacrifice the rest of her days to the care of her children and the scars that she insisted had been cut into them by the war.

Tetty and Malcolm, though, had suffered few such traumas. The girl had turned inward and, with her grandmother's help, had nurtured herself with books and plans of one day traveling to Paris. As she had grown in both height and depth, she had become almost as serious as the retired teacher and had even taken to calling her "Martha" when she let her. Her brother had fared even better. Rubbery and inexhaustible, he had defied the air raids and the daily privations with his own boy's stratagems, hollering and mysterious stones and codes spelled out with shoes. Everyone had marveled at his courage, forgetting perhaps that children are brave mostly because their total helplessness requires them to be.

Yet tonight Malcolm alarmed even his grandmother when he suddenly turned toward her in the dark and whispered, "I lost a friend of mine last week."

It was her custom during these visits to lie next to the children until they drifted off, then slip out into the kitchen to have some tea with their parents and to call Samuel. The old woman no longer cared for sleep. It simply wearied her with more dreams.

"That's a pity," Martha whispered back so as not to awaken his less restive sister. "Did you quarrel or were you only playing at hide-and-seek?"

"No," the boy corrected her. "I mean he died. He'd been hurt years ago by the Germans, and he never really got any better. Then he didn't come around anymore. Then he quit school and church. Then they told us." The voice from beneath the counterpane shrank and broke. "I was only wondering if you knew if we *have* to go to heaven when we die. Father hasn't much interest in such things, and Mother . . ."

He trailed off, and Martha quickly tried to reassure him that his friend must be at peace. "Sometimes," she finished, "when people can't mend completely, rest is best, I think. But wouldn't you want him to be there now, where you could meet up with him again, eventually?"

Malcolm thought about this for a time, then confided in her, "I'd rather not. I miss the days when we used to run up and down the streets together and climb the fences at the factory and meet at the pylons down by the river and stay out long after our mothers called us in. That was heaven to Alan and me, Grandmother." He sighed as he finally closed his eyes.

Once Martha heard both children breathing regularly, she went to sit with her son and his wife. They talked in muted tones on harmless topics, as the winter night closed in upon them. In the darkness, Dorothy's melancholy infected the entire room, and soon they decided to turn in early. Paul told his mother that he would drive her back home the following afternoon, then he kissed her good night.

Before going to bed, Martha used the telephone and waited to hear her husband's distant voice. But no one answered, even though the switchboard operator promised her there was nothing wrong with the lines. Time and again, she tried to get through, only to imagine the empty parlor, the instrument jangling madly in its cradle, and poor Samuel dying or worse in the upstairs bedroom. Surely, she thought, it was too late and cold for him to be still lingering at the Fountain Inn pub or on his way back home. And then she had such a lurid vision of him fallen and frozen in the snow that she dropped the handset and started at the loud crack it made when it struck the marble tabletop.

Wars and losses had robbed Martha of most of her original faith, yet at times like these she still liked to offer up a silent prayer for those she loved. In her case, however, she usually addressed the nearest streetlamp with a few words of supplication, as if light itself could somehow save them all from ruin.

The next morning, Martha went along with Dorothy to the local shops while she waited for the hour of her departure. She did so more out of a sense of duty than desire, most of her attention now being directed toward Hedge End and Samuel's continuing silence. After she rose, she had rung their home number repeatedly without success, until she'd wondered if she shouldn't try to contact Dr. Little, Rebecca Pye, or even Franklin Pratt, the boot maker who acted as the village's unelected constable. If any of them could only look in on her husband and tell her he was well, then perhaps she might finally swallow the hard knot in her throat and quiet the tripping of her heart.

Now she followed along behind the younger woman from street to street, too distracted by all that had happened in the past few weeks to pay much attention to what her daughter-in-law was saying.

"Do you see what I was telling you?" Dorothy nervously flung the words back over her shoulder. "Do you see what the war's done to us? Here it is, already three years on, and most of the neighborhood is still recovering. These piles of rubble, that broken standpipe, all the children looking so underfed — none of this will ever be the same again in our lifetimes. Never!"

Martha looked about her, but she couldn't see it. What she noticed more than anything else was how different winter in a city was from winter in a village. Here was a peculiar cold, a taste of chromium in the air that wasn't altogether unpleasant, as well as light that had more steel and electricity in it than sun. The flow of road traffic took the place of wind through trees in Hedge End, and gutters mimicked streams so perfectly that she could hardly tell the one from the other. Martha had never been able to understand those people who ranted either against large cities or small towns. To her, they were merely like two different children, like Tetty and Malcolm, the hamlet introspective and inclined toward murmurs and the metropolis as rambunctious as a colt in a paddock. To prefer one over the other was absurd. It was only a question of energy, which, as one grew older, naturally fell off and made an exile in the countryside seem more practical.

After meeting her grandchildren for lunch at a shop near their school, Martha came back to the barber's until Paul finished for the day. She was hoping that the meditative rhythms of stropping and scraping and clipping would calm her some, and they did. Even the lazy, erratic discourse of the men waiting for shaves and trims helped her put Samuel's absence in perspective and set aside for now her other preoccupations. Only in the last hour of the afternoon did the talk turn somewhat darker.

Out of one of the meringue cones of towels lying back in a chair came a voice that said, "Well, the only thing I know is that I saw it coming long before it did, and so should have everyone else."

"What's that?" asked another.

"Oh, that whole India thing last month, the killing of that Gandhi fellow and all the rest of it." The customer snorted and automatically pulled down his vest to cover his paunch. "It's a fact of life, though, isn't it?" he went on. "Whenever people are let loose before they're ready, they maffick about like a pack of hyenas smelling blood. We should have never done an about-turn and pulled out of there before the coolies had a substitute structure of their own in place. It was just bad policy. And, given the fact that none of them had ever had any experience in governing before, they must have been mad to think they could take over what we'd left them. Stark staring."

A man in the waiting chair next to Martha's sofa spoke up. "They're smaller than we are, too, aren't they?" he said to the room. "Physically, that is. Most of them."

"How could that matter?"

"And it only stands to reason," he continued, "that people of that size can't manage the buildings and the machinery that had been designed for whites. Their hands won't fit. They seem a bit simple, too, as if they're short on nutrition. Being small-boned and vegetarian, the way they all are." He shivered with disgust.

"No, no, no." A third man lifted the corner of the apron that protected his suit and pointed with an unlit cigarette. "It's not their individual proportions that's the problem, it's their national mix. They've so many races and languages and religions over there, not to mention far too high a birth-rate, that it's impossible for them to work together. It's the same as we were here before the Union, only ten times worse. And with their abysmal level of poverty!"

An idle discussion ensued in which the two men under towels held forth for a purely political analysis, while the man nearest Martha muttered on about skin colors and the shapes of heads. The exchange was typical barber's shop debate, which meant that it signified little more than a haphazard group of strangers talking in their sleep.

Finally, the first man began again, in an effort to reclaim the theme that he clearly thought of as his. "Now I'm not saying this Gandhi wasn't enough of a clever Dick in his own way. He was that, and not by halves. Still" — he gestured by pointing the snout of his towel — "anyone in his position should have seen the troubles coming, the tensions between the Hindus and the Muslims, the breaking away of Pakistan, the rioting. He should have known that, under certain circumstances, people like that simply can't be trusted with so much freedom. It just isn't natural."

Sitting in a haze of sunlight through the pebbled window, Martha felt that she could hold back no longer. But, just as she was preparing her objections, she was interrupted by the voice of her son, raised in mannerly protest.

"I always thought freedom was an absolute," Paul said, his lather brush clogged in its mug. He looked straight at his mother as he asked the other men, "Besides, how could any human being ever have too much liberty?"

Later, on their walk around the corner to the garage where Paul stored his 1929 Morris Minor, he asked his mother very carefully, "I don't suppose, then, that I should be expecting any more letters from India for you? The last one came with the New Year, but —"

"No," Martha said. "No more letters. That's all over with now."

Night fell before the old woman reached Hedge End and her misplaced husband, or at least there was enough despondency and fear surrounding her to be mistaken for night.

4

SATURDAYS FOR THE HOUGHTONS were days given over to dawdling, especially in the mornings. They had their tea and Chelsea buns in bed, later tucked their nightshirts about their legs in the flowered chairs that were used for nothing else, and took up books and catalogs that had been stoutly left unread all week. Conversation was kept to a minimum, for at this point in their marriage even talking to each other had become almost as superfluous as talking to oneself. Yet this particular Saturday was different.

So far this morning, Samuel hadn't said a word about his wife's late arrival last night or her frantic telephoning. He'd said hardly anything, but had merely studied his motor journals. At first, Martha put it down to the usual seasonal dejection that afflicted him at this same time every year. Her husband had never borne their winters very well. He missed the damp winds of spring and summer's green heat, and even the light of autumn, as thin as tissue, soothed him like beer. But, as the morning progressed, Martha began to think that something more was at work here than just the cold and the snow. Samuel Houghton had never been known as much of a talker. Anyone in Botley or Hedge End could attest to that. Yet today his silences seemed more deliberate than ever.

"So you *were* at home, then?" she asked him again as she brought up some fresh toast from the kitchen. "All Thursday night and Friday morning when I was ringing you every minute on the minute and making myself sick with worry?"

"Mmm-mmm."

"Why didn't you answer, then? What is it you were so busy doing," she demanded querulously, "that you couldn't have picked up the receiver and let me know you were all right?"

"Sleeping, I expect. Or fussing with something out in the shed."

"Then —" Martha halted, suddenly at a loss. She resented the way Samuel was so unfairly spoiling their Saturday morning together. Even though, with neither of them working anymore, they were rarely out of each other's sight for the rest of the week, Saturday was still supposed to be their best day. In the short reach of the village and all its ever present neighbors, such precious respites were hard enough to come by. Gazing at her husband over the top edge of her newspaper, Martha recalled having read that William Blake and his wife, Catherine, used to sit together naked in their enclosed Lambeth garden like Adam and Eve. Not that the Houghtons would have ever forgotten themselves to the point of licensing such behavior. Yet sometimes Martha found herself missing the shorter, quicker days of their courtship and early marriage, when every word and look and touch of hand had shivered with newness and infinite discovery. In her younger years, she'd always imagined that old age somehow compensated one for the loss of novelty with a greater joy in the familiar, the serene. But she had not been here then.

An alder branch just below the bedroom window abruptly sprang upward as if from the launch of a bird, yet the cause was only a sheath of ice, crackling off.

"Still," she repeated her grievance, "you might have had the decency to listen for my call or even ring me yourself at Paul's. At our age, Samuel, neither of us knows the day or the hour. We might be carried off at any time, and then where's the other? We're not apart often or for very long, but when we are I think we should try our best to keep in touch. Otherwise, there's no telling what mischief might befall us."

Because there was really nothing her husband could say to this, his silence wasn't open to rebuke. But Martha couldn't rest until she had elicited an appropriate response from him.

"Promise me, at least, that from this moment on," she persevered, "we'll not lose contact for such a long time as we did the other night. Do this for me, Samuel, so I shouldn't ever have to suffer such a horrid fright again. Unless," she added hopefully, "you'd care to talk to me a little more about this."

Across from her, Samuel peeked up from his journal, an expression of honest wonder on his face, or it might have been only impatience. "Talk?"

Most of the day passed in the same cool manner. Samuel kept himself to his accustomed circuit, clattering about in the shed out back or napping in his chair by the fire. Martha stayed mostly in the kitchen at the window, whose light she favored for reading and knitting. None of this was different from any of their other thousands of Saturdays together. But, to Martha's mind, there was a brittleness between them that hadn't been there in decades — not, perhaps, since their first tentative days as lovers. She couldn't account for it, other than to put it down to the dulling effects of the gray skies and their combined years. That the surprise letter from India might have had some part in the change never occurred to her. Samuel was far too wise and understanding a man ever to allow something so slight to come between them.

In the evening, the Houghtons were obliged to go out, whatever their humor or the season. Two Saturdays a month in Hedge End were reserved for the Darby and Joan Club that had recently been inaugurated for the local elderly after Lord Soulbury's Streatham model of a few years earlier. Held by rotation in the homes of the two dozen or so members, the gathering was a smoky and talc-scented night of whist, small talk, frothing waves of silver hair, and malacca canes dangling from pegs. As tea trolleys circulated through the rooms, seemingly under their own power, the older villagers traded memories back and forth like so many tricks and nodded over how much had been lost to time. Their status as survivors, especially after the last war, drew them closer together into a fraternity that warmed them, inside and out. Nowadays, such assemblies were becoming more and more necessary, as their children and their grandchildren continued to wander off toward the larger cities and fewer young families chose the village as a place to plan their futures.

Given her passion for organizing, Rebecca Pye should have been the most obvious choice as the founder of such a club. But, although she was indeed the first to sign up, the initiative belonged to another. Rival Cobb was a widower in his eighties who lived in a stone bungalow beside the kissing gate near Upper Northam Road. A resident of the village for no more than twenty years, he was a proud and proper old gentleman, never to be caught out of his neckcloth and trilby hat, whose squared shoulders and wedge-shaped face could be seen in any street at any hour. He contributed observations and reviews to the local and regional newspapers, but whether his writings constituted a new hobby or the outcome of a journalistic career was unknown. The chatter of his typewriter could be heard through his open window even in the deep of night, to be followed the next day by duplicates that had been painstakingly pecked out for anyone who wanted them. Some Hedge Enders supposed that Cobb had started the club only to have a steady supply of editorial copy, but others more generously proposed loneliness as his primary motive and came to keep him company.

In the past, Martha remembered, Samuel had expressed only disdain for the fortnightly meetings and their participants. "Nothing but a circle of sorry dears," he'd complained, "wittering endlessly on about who's got what sort of growth on what and where what's-his-name wants to be planted when his time comes. Hasn't anyone in this village anything better to do?" Yet tonight he himself proved to be more animated than ever before. He rushed ahead of his wife into the drawing room and immediately reserved two chairs at the loudest, most long-winded of all the card tables. Mr. and Mrs. Eaton, with their burgundy complexions and their horse teeth, had traveled simply everywhere, left their initials on an alphabetical list of the world's monuments, and had the photographs to prove it. Before, Samuel had diligently avoided their presence. But now he sought them out and encouraged them to tell him the same tired tales that he'd already heard only the month before.

Even Rita Venden, the youngest club member, who recorded a weekly *Garden Paths* program for the BBC and raised nothing but weeds, noticed the difference in him.

"Say, your old fellow is certainly doing himself up smart this evening," she remarked to Martha over a platter of cheeses. "I don't think I've ever seen him acting so brisk. Are you, by chance, slipping anything special into his feed?"

Others agreed. Rival Cobb praised Samuel's renewed energy, the postman said he envied him his wit, while Jane Adderley, the crippled woman who raised herbs and radishes under glass, thought he was someone else altogether. And Rebecca Pye, toward the end of the festivities, wondered how she could have been so wrong about her best friend's husband.

"He's been as gabby as a magpie tonight!" she cried across the mound of coats on the bed. "I'd never have suspected Samuel to be such a raconteur. Not at his age."

What else could Martha say, but that she, too, found it most extraordinary?

After the night at the club, it was clear to Martha that her husband, like some pouting child, was refusing to speak only to her. Except for the compulsory replies to inquiries about her reading glasses and what would he like to eat tonight, Samuel maintained a stubborn aloofness. He seemed always to be moving out of whichever room she was moving into, or he was conveniently too far away to make out what she was asking him. From outside, anyone looking in might have thought they were trying to catch up to each other from floor to floor of their house, when exactly the reverse was true.

He'd worked this ploy often enough before. Brooding wordlessness had usually been his weapon of choice in their long marriage. Martha's was a burst of manic activity, teaching and errands and bouts of cleaning that drowned out all of her spouse's efforts to make peace in their infrequent fights over child-rearing, finances, or mutual friends. She considered his methods to be immature, while he thought of hers as heartless. But, overall, the Houghtons had managed to build between them a working dynamic that suited them about as well as anything could. "Flexibility is the key," they had many times told younger, jittery couples who wished to know their secret. "Giving way isn't the same as giving in." Home truths like these, scratched for and won after long uphill climbs, were what had allowed Martha and Samuel to survive their own worst habits and still sleep side by side.

Nevertheless, by Thursday, Martha was so upset by the house's new monastic stillness that she decided to cancel her weekly visit to Southampton and seek advice in Hedge End instead. Confronting Samuel directly was out of the question. That would have wounded her pride, and besides she was half afraid of hearing what he might have to say. Martha's second option was a stop at Dr. Little's clinic in St. John's Road. He'd been settled there for nearly four years now and, as a veteran of the India Medical Service, seemed to offer her an ideal halfway point between her past memories of Gandhi and her present troubles with Samuel. She rarely came to see the doctor herself, following a primitive urge to cure most diseases by not admitting their symptoms. This notion had failed her more than once — the appendicitis during the early years of her marriage, the "change" during the latter — but sheer good fortune had carried her through the rest, all the flu and the polio epidemics that had scarred so much of the century. Now she regarded Dr. Little more as a family friend, a pub mate of her husband's, than as a professional whose expertise was as open to hire as any gardener's.

Which was more or less how he welcomed her into his consulting room today. "You say there's something off with

Samuel?" he began. "I wonder that he doesn't come in to see me himself."

"But you know how he always likes to hear your diagnoses of him through me first. So I was thinking that perhaps you might be able to tell me what's wrong with him even before he can."

This much was true. After an examination or a blood sample, Samuel preferred to use Martha as a filter through which the good or bad news could be leaked out to him gently and dismissively. It was one of the Houghtons' secrets, one which Samuel was sure all the other men of the village would ridicule him for if they knew, though more than one of them used the same or a similar ploy in their own private lives.

As Dr. Little frowned across his desk at his visitor, Martha took stock of the room that she'd been in only a few times before. The doctor's travels could be charted on his walls, but what Martha was most interested in were his memorabilia from India. These objects held places of honor and were thoughtfully labeled, unlike the more commercial pieces that Rebecca Pye specialized in. Portraits on burlap of leonine gods glaring out from symmetrical typhoons of colors and designs hung above an oxidized bronze statue of a four-armed Siva in a circle of flames, posed on one leg upon a sleeping child. In a hushed corner sat a Buddha of red sandstone, his left hand holding a begging bowl in his lap and his right touching the earth to summon it to witness his breakthrough enlightenment. Martha was reminded of a brief postal dalliance she'd had back in the twenties with the fledgling Buddhist Society of London and of the great peacefulness it had brought her for a time. How was it possible, she asked herself now, to lose wisdom even after she had attained it? But that was one of those spiritual matters that she had always looked to Gandhi to answer for her, as he had looked to her to help guide him through dress codes and English table etiquette and remedies for unintended affronts to his loved ones. And now neither of them could ask the other anything.

"I'm afraid I don't understand," Dr. Little said to bring her eyes back to him.

"Nor do I." Martha smiled then and went on less cryptically, "It's only that Samuel's been so moody of late. I don't know what to do with him. It's not that he's underfoot or anything about the house, but quite the contrary. He's standoffish and surly, and he has hardly a good word to say to me from morning till night. It's all I can do to get him to speak my name."

"And how long has this been going on?"

"Only a few days, but —"

"Has he sustained any head injury?" asked the doctor, flourishing over a notepad a sparkling new Biro that must have been the first of its kind in Hedge End. "Any headaches, slurred speech, confusion? Has he fallen recently, or have you noticed that he's begun to drop things or forget what day it is?"

"No, no." Martha sighed in exasperation. "It's nothing of the sort. I hate to admit it, but perhaps it's rather less of a physical and more of a personal matter between us. The fact is, doctor, I suspect he's horribly angry with me, and I have no idea what might have caused it. At least, I don't think I do."

The man spread his hands as if in surrender. "In that case, the best prescription I can give you is time. We all become more intractable as we get older, more prone to feeling every slight against us and to holding meaningless grudges longer. Even we medicos, I'm sorry to say, aren't immune to such temporary fits of ill humor." He sat back in the uncertain light from the window and tried to console Martha, who continued to scan the room. "Unless you can think of any specific problem between you and your husband that I might counsel you about, I don't see how I —"

"There is something."

At any other time, Martha never would have considered revealing anything about her early experiences in Portsmouth or last week's desperate letter from Bombay or anything in between. It was risky enough to have taken Rebecca Pye into her confidence during all these years, though little of what the outlandish bookseller said was believed by most of the village. Dr. Little, on the other hand, was revered by one and all, and he was famous for his ready conversation. Even with the best will in the world, she worried, he might let something slip that would only embarrass her and anger Samuel even further.

But Gandhi's death and his son's dying and Samuel's frustrating remoteness had left her without much choice, and she told the doctor as much as she dared. As with Rebecca Pye, his look registered the breathless shock of one who finds himself in the presence of reflected fame.

"You don't tell me?" he mused. "Imagine that! Perhaps, then, poor Samuel is simply feeling a bit jealous."

"Jealous? Of what?"

"Well, of your superior worldliness. You've known, haven't you, one of the most celebrated men of our time, if not of all time? This is something that an ironmonger from Botley might well envy in his wife. I feel some of the same myself," he said with a modest laugh, "directed against me by my fellow Hedge Enders for my world travels. As much as we cherish our homes and our cozy village lives, Mrs. Houghton, the horizons do begin to shrink in on us as the years pass. Most likely, Samuel's only feeling daunted by all that you've seen and heard."

"But I've never *been* anywhere," Martha protested, "certainly never out of England. It was Samuel who went to Flanders for the first show, and they even ferried him over once toward the end of the last. London's the farthest I've ever been, and that only a handful of times. If anyone should be jealous, I suppose it should be me."

"But what about here and here?" Dr. Little indicated his heart and his head, though it took Martha a few moments to understand his gestures. "It may be that he resents the mere exposure, the chances you've had to savor other, distant worlds, while he was condemned to stay behind. You say you spent only a day or two with Gandhi some sixty years ago, but isn't childhood the very time when our strongest bonds are forged? I expect Samuel only wishes that he'd been able to have some friendship half as exotic and renowned."

"Still," Martha mumbled evasively, "it's not as if it went on for any length of time."

Not hearing her, the doctor nodded toward a scroll painting that showed a line of profiles making for a blue pool marked "Manasarovar, the Lake of the Mind."

"Pilgrimages, you see," he said with a trace of longing, "needn't always be through foreign lands. Sometimes sitting quietly in a chair can take you the farthest away. And now, with all your unique memories having been reawakened by this letter from India, you seemed to have outstripped your husband even in that."

Dissatisfied with the consultation, Martha headed for the Olympia and Rebecca Pye's more sympathetic ear. But today the bookshop was not the same private haven as the week before. Thursdays were school days, when Martha's successors at the National School shepherded in waddling bundles of scarves and mittens to browse among the treasures that so few of them could afford. The boys steered at once for Bevis and Sexton Blake, while the girls preferred *The Would-be-goods* and George MacDonald. Yet, perhaps unnoticed by the children and certainly by their parents, Rebecca liked to seed their reading with characters from the various Jataka tales and the *Ramayana,* as well as with a simplified version of the *Bhagavad Gita.* This she did, not out of any real desire to convert them, but out of respect for a sacred history from which her own life's circumstances had excluded her.

The children filed in from the icy cold and carried floating mists in their mouths and in the folds of their coats. As Martha made her way through their enthusiasm, she wondered again what must be wrong with those fogeys who couldn't tolerate the young. She knew so many like that, most of the lot at their Saturday night club, even Samuel on his worst days. They pined for a past that had no substance outside of recollection, and they somehow blamed children for embracing the same youthful spirit their elders had wasted or discarded. Martha had never seen it in that way. To her, nothing could ever take the place of beginnings. At seventy-two, she would gladly have become a child all over again.

As soon as Rebecca saw her, she came across the room and said, "What? No Southampton today?"

"I thought not. The weather," Martha replied offhandedly. "And Samuel's not feeling at all himself."

"Really? But he seemed perfectly fit to me the other night. In rare form, I thought."

"He hides it well."

The presence of the excited schoolchildren prevented the two women from speaking as freely as they might have wished. But, for Martha, there was also the greater restraint of not wanting to admit to any problems, especially to someone who took so much pride in being an expert on problematic marriages. In addition, many people assumed that anything as long-lived as the Houghtons' union must be perfect, and disabusing them of this illusion had often made Martha feel that she was somehow letting them down.

"Perhaps Dr. Little —" Rebecca began.

"No, I've just come from there." Martha followed her to a far corner of the shop, from where they could watch the whirlpool of young readers in comparative safety. "He seems to think that Samuel's behavior might have something to do with jealousy," she continued. "I think it's absurd myself, at this late stage, but he claims that even older men can feel that their lives haven't been all that they should have been."

"What's wrong with him? Samuel, I mean."

"Oh, he's been so quiet and unresponsive and dreary that it's like living with a stone. Do you know what he did yesterday, or was it the day before?" asked Martha. "He spent the entire afternoon sitting in a chair across from me, and not once — not one single blessed time! — did he ever talk to me or answer my questions. I thought I'd lost my hearing, as silent and dull as the room was. Now you tell me," she said to her friend. "You tell me if that's any decent way for a man to treat his wife of forty-eight years."

There was always some hazard involved with asking Rebecca Pye anything about husbands. Hedge End rumor had it that both of her first two had gone to war mainly for some peace and quiet and that the third lived in hope of another world conflict. Marketing words as she did had rendered her extravagant with her own, and by now she was frankly incapable of understanding anyone who bothered to breathe without saying something.

"But you said Dr. Little mentioned that Samuel might be jealous," she reminded Martha. "Yet of whom? There are so few men left about who are still moving. Is it Mr. Cobb he was thinking of?" she cried suddenly, a flare of light coming on in her eyes. "He *is* a goer, though, isn't he? Did you see how fine his hands looked at the Darby and Joan the other night? Liver-spotted and gnarled, yes, but still —"

"Not of him, Rebecca," Martha interrupted her. "But of, well, of that time down in Portsmouth."

This news was altogether too much for the bookseller. "Are these men in their best minds? That was a lifetime ago, two lifetimes, when you were nothing but a silly little chit of a girl and the master was a saint in the making. And which of us remembers what we did that far back anyway, or why? If every man and woman were held to account for all their past actions," she stated with a horrified expression, ignoring her own philosophy, "none of us would have the time or the courage to do anything in the future.

"Besides," she resumed after running off to exchange some issues of *Modern Boy* for a palmful of money, "if your Samuel were feeling anything of the sort, I'm sure he would never have come in here and wasted most of a day trying to find out as much as he could about both Gandhi and India."

Martha stared at her, and said, "What? When was this?"

"This day last week, while you were off visiting Paul. In comes Samuel with the first sun," Rebecca set the scene with a smirk, "as busy and jolly as you please, as if he hadn't been avoiding me and my shop all these years. 'The Indian,' he says to me. 'The one who just got himself shot. How much do you have on him?' What else could I do?" Rebecca shrugged. "I directed him toward that special display over there and let him have at it."

"How long was he here?"

"Oh, for hours, hours."

Martha glanced at the display of books, then at the schoolchildren who were still peering over one another's shoulders, then at the changing colors of the street outside.

"What did he find?" she said at last. "Did he happen to say?"

"He kept himself very close," the bookseller recalled with a conspiratorial nudge. "He hadn't a word to spare me after that, though I did come up to him once or twice to offer my help. I promised him that no one in Hedge End, excepting yourself, had a better understanding of the India situation or Mr. Gandhi in particular. I remember your telling me last week," she whispered in her own defense, "that you'd already gone ahead and let him know all about Portsmouth, so I thought there was no harm in my saying anything. But your Samuel didn't seem much interested in what anyone else knew. Not a bit of it. He only wanted to be left alone to crouch over book after book and stand there steaming in his greatcoat while the rest of my customers had to part their way around him."

"Did he buy anything?" wondered Martha.

"Not so much as a newspaper," Rebecca complained with a shopkeeper's bitterness. "And this after spending half the day, scribbling notes on the back of an envelope and copying out dates from one of the new chronologies of the master's life."

"Which one was that? Can you show me?"

Rebecca led her friend across the room to a volume that had just arrived from Calcutta. Martha cracked open the warped boards, noted the publisher's emblem of hook-and-eye characters and counterclockwise swastikas, and shifted slightly aside to thumb through its pages. The other woman continued to talk, but her visitor was too immersed in reading to respond, and eventually Rebecca moved off to barter with the teachers from the National School. Standing perhaps in the same tense posture that her husband had assumed a week earlier, Martha pored through the book as if Samuel's eyes must have left some traces of their passing, some sign of hurt or anger that she might be able to recognize. But, in the end, she still couldn't guess at what her husband had or had not learned during his uncharacteristic stop at the Olympia.

"You're off out, then?" Rebecca called as she watched the retired teacher being swept toward the door by the exiting schoolchildren. "Do you have any idea what Samuel was looking for in here?"

"None," Martha answered from the midst of all the small bodies. "But I'm sure he'll find some way to tell me in his own good time."

Outside, the winter dusk made her feel paradoxically even more lively than the bookshop had. The sharpness of the air and the mica light seemed to broaden her vision, until the village and her place in it settled into a just and timeless symmetry. If it hadn't been for the paralyzing weariness that came over her as she turned down her own road, she might have felt younger than she had in years.

When she finally reached home, Martha paused at the door, bracing herself again for Samuel's new silence. But she needn't have bothered. She could tell at once that the house was empty, both below and above. They had lived here together long enough for each of them to be able to detect the absence of the other. Tonight there was no one waiting for her anywhere.

"Samuel," she called out without any hope of an answer. "Might I talk to you for a moment?"

It was not until Martha entered the kitchen that she knew

something had changed, something was wrong. There, meticulously arranged across the table's blue-checked oilcloth, lay a strange assortment of items, most of which she hadn't seen in years.

A ceramic plate from Shelton's Vegetarian Hotel, 25 Madeira Road, Ventnor, Isle of Wight.

An ancient address book whose spine bore the faded legend of the Cecil Hotel in London.

Colored prints of the façades of the Holborn Restaurant at Holborn and Kingsway and the Criterion in Piccadilly Circus.

A long-lost volume, Tolstoy's *The Kingdom of God Is Within You,* with — as a forgotten bookmark in the center — a ticket to a meeting of the West London Ethical Society at 45 Queens Road, Bayswater, dated 18 July 1909.

A tarnished spoon stamped with the insignia of Netley Hospital.

The sheet music and libretto for Gustav Holst's *Choral Hymns from the Rig Veda* out of the library of one George Bell.

Martha stood for the longest while, mesmerized by the exhibit set out before her. At first, in a fit of panic, she imagined that all these mementos and purchases had somehow gathered here on the kitchen table of their own accord. They had crept out of wardrobes and from under chairs and cabinets, they had rolled down the stairs and negotiated corners, they had magically congregated after having marched in single file through the entire house. Even once she'd pictured Samuel spending days, ferreting out such meaningless odds and ends from dusty trunks and drawers, she still couldn't comprehend why. Was he growing so senile that this is how he amused himself while she was out, constructing mad, runic designs from household belongings? Or was there some more sinister meaning behind them, some riddle to be deciphered? No small amount of time passed before Martha finally succeeded in reading the message correctly. And then she lowered herself heavily into one of the chairs and wondered what on earth she had done.

A few hours later, she was still staring at the table, waiting for the sound of her husband's hand at the front door. Never before had she heard such quiet. The house, the street, the village, the stars — all stood motionless. The slush of her own blood in her ears and the even fainter hum of her nerves signaled the only life in the house. Her plan was to sit on here until Samuel returned, no matter how late it might be, and shame him for worrying her so, before she tried to explain. But, as she was later to learn, he was already too far away for that.

5

MARTHA TURNED first to Franklin Pratt for help. In the floury confines of her kitchen, the boot maker's hobnailed footwear seemed to take up most of the floor. "Now you tell me that your husband was here in the house as recently as last night?" he asked her, gripping a pencil stump above his notebook.

"I presume so. At least, there was evidence to that effect."

"Evidence, you say? What manner of evidence would that be?"

Martha gazed down at the oilcloth between them, now littered with nothing more mysterious than coffee stains and plates dusted with toast crumbs. Constable Pratt — so he was called by most of Hedge End, though he himself disavowed the title — had insisted on only the same midmorning breakfast that he'd enjoyed all his life. "I could eat toast five or six times a day, and have," he had promised her. "There's that much glorious variety in it."

"Nothing, really," Martha now hurried to assure him,

ushering the tableware off to one side. "You know, only the sort of household articles that let one know someone else is about. You must understand this as well as I. How long have *you* been married?"

"Mrs. Pratt has kindly endured my company, madam, for near on eleven years now, and I hope to impose upon her good graces for thrice eleven more." A mewing, boyish look came over his hard-boned face as he lovingly thought of the woman, a third his size, who — depending on whom one listened to — was either too giddy or too solemn for him. "But was there nothing left out or behind," he went on, his pencil held eagerly ready, "that might lead you to believe your husband had departed in a hurry or was, perhaps, surprised by some third party? No breakage, no visible changes, nothing of great value missing? Even in a hamlet as peaceful as this one, we've had our share of robberies. And worse!"

"No, not at all." Martha shook her head. "Here in the kitchen, where I'd come to look for him first thing, I found a few objects that I hadn't seen in a while — a plate, some books, a photograph or two. But those are just the kinds of items that are pulled out of a drawer or a wardrobe when you're trying to find something else. Or," she added more thoughtfully, "things you've taken for granted all your life that suddenly acquire a new significance from some casual word or event. You know what it is to grow older, Constable. How much of one's past lies about in ever growing piles, how easy it is to forget what you'd once promised yourself to remember forever."

Pratt nodded sympathetically and said, "I do, indeed. But to continue. You have, of course, already rung around to your family and to most of his usual haunts, tried to trace the route he would normally have taken today if he were out?"

"Of course. The children, Dr. Little's, the chemist's, the pubs, his friends. I even rang the marine shop in Bursledon Road that used to be his, but no one's seen or heard from him in days. I'm sure it's nothing, really, only an old woman's bother. But I'd feel so much better if I could only find out where he's got to and if he's all right and on his way back home to me. And I didn't know whom else to ask."

Pratt slowly uncrossed, then recrossed, his legs, an elaborate undertaking that involved labored breathing and a vicious kick to an empty chair. The maneuver reminded Martha of her husband's work with the floating cranes at the Southampton docks during the war. How had they ever managed to come so far and still be so frightfully unlike each other? And how had she and Gandhi managed to achieve the exact opposite, while most of the time being half a world apart?

Pratt leaned closer. "You'll forgive me, Mrs. Houghton." He sighed. "But it's part of my duties to ask. You and your husband, now. You haven't been having any special difficulties lately? Any words or arguments that might have driven him away or off on his own to do something — tragic?"

"Goodness, no!" Martha shivered in spite of the oven, propped open with a glove, which spread a quilt of heat across the room. "We've had our spats, like any other couple, a new one just this past week, as a matter of fact. But Samuel's too sensible a man ever to attempt anything so — I don't know — theatrical. He's got more than his fair portion of pride, and sometimes he tries to do more than he's able. Yet I've never known him to give up on any struggle before it's finished.

"No," she informed the scribbling constable, "what I'm more afraid of is that he's fallen somewhere, unconscious, and the cold might be starting to get at him. Don't you remember ten, fifteen years ago, Mr. Pratt? That poor Fenwick girl who stumbled on her way home from the grocer's and struck her head on a stone and froze to death by morning? And she was only a child. I can't bear to think what might have happened to a man Samuel's age, out alone at night in such weather and with lungs like his. He'd be fortunate if he came away with nothing worse than pneumonia."

As genuine as her concern was, there was a part of Martha that harbored an even deeper fear, that Samuel, instead of being the victim of some mischance, was fit and happy and with all his faculties intact, but simply gone.

"I know Hedge End hasn't any true constabulary force to speak of," resumed Martha as delicately as she could and cringed at Pratt's reddening cheeks. "But is there anything you can do to help me through this? Can word be got out somehow?"

"Steps have already been taken," he informed her and pocketed his notebook. "I notified my colleagues in Botley and Southampton as soon as you rang me this morning, and since then I've talked to most of our own shopkeepers and neighbors. The villagers will keep a watch for him on the streets, and the closest farmers — you know the Webbs and the Tallards, don't you, down by the banks of the Hamble? — are going to walk their fields today before nightfall. If your man's anywhere about," he said with a tap on the table, "well or ill, we'll find him, or we'll know the reason why he's gone missing. You can depend upon that, Mrs. Houghton."

As Pratt rose to his feet, he commented that at least, this time, it was an adult they were looking for, and not some lost child. Martha agreed, though within her she thought differently. Now, for the first time in her and Samuel's long life together, she realized that, once the children were gone, she'd begun to coddle and tolerate him almost as if he were her second surviving son. And, as she accompanied Pratt to the door, it occurred to her, again for perhaps the first time, that her husband might not have been altogether pleased with such treatment.

Once more alone in the kitchen, to occupy her mind, Martha took from a curtained shelf a box containing the assorted objects that Samuel had used as his parting note to her. Most of them she set aside, but she lingered a bit longer over the music by Holst. The booklet's paper was powdery with neglect and bore the marks of every one of its forty-some years. An odor of decay hung over the pages, as it did, Martha was forced to concede, over much of the house around her. Leafing through the book, she remembered more clearly how she had come by the score. It had been in the autumn of 1931, and she and Samuel had traveled to Chichester to visit their daughter Alice. While her daughter and husband had gone shopping, Martha had toured the cathedral and the Market Cross. The usual Saturday crowds had been somewhat thinned by the economic crisis that was slowly spreading outward from America, and on the Continent inchoate rumblings from a newcomer named Hitler were already making themselves heard. But Martha had still taken advantage of the weekend away from her Hedge End school to marvel at the church's late Gothic choir screen and the Norman stone panel depicting the raising of Lazarus. Eventually, she had even been introduced to the bishop of Chichester, Dr. George Bell, and had joined him for a sherry in his overstocked library. And it was there, because she said she'd always admired it, that he had given her a copy of his old friend's music, never dreaming that he should miss it three years later when he laid the composer's ashes to rest beneath the floor of his own north transept.

With the kitchen growing increasingly warm and sleepy,

Martha's eyes fell upon an isolated stanza at the close of the "Hymn to Manas":

> O thou who hast fled away
> To be united with the All that is, and is to be.
> We call thee back to dwell with us again.

In a sudden fit of anxiety, she asked herself which of the two men in her life she was missing more, Gandhi or Samuel. And her inability to come up with an answer left her sitting before the box of objects for hours without really seeing any of them.

"You want us to do what?" Rebecca asked that afternoon.

"I want our church choir to put on an evening of selections from this," Martha repeated with a nod at the musical score lying on the table between them. "Only two or three of the hymns, perhaps, to commemorate Gandhi's passing. It shouldn't prove too far beyond their skills, and I can't imagine that we don't have enough musicians to keep up with us. It'd surely be no more troublesome, would it, than that Bach cantata we tried last year?"

"I know the work, of course. I may have even heard it sung some time or other, in whole or in part. But, my dear," Rebecca went on, glancing worriedly about, "passions are still running fairly high over the India question, and even the master's death hasn't done much to stem that. I don't question your grief or your principles — I'd never dare — but I am concerned about how our neighbors might react. Don't you think it's still too early in the day for this sort of general, public demonstration?"

The two women were sitting at a window table in the Eglantine, the decorated parlor that passed for Hedge End's main tearoom. It was run by Emily Quinn, a woman in her mid-thirties whose husband's dream of becoming a freelance inventor had driven them with their three children out of pricey Bath and into the countryside. While Mr. Quinn and his son busied themselves in a back room with unscaled sketches and models of balsa wood, his wife and sometimes his two daughters served homemade seed cakes, puddings, and chamomile tea in an artificial atmosphere of rose chintz curtains and bentwood chairs that was half drawing room and half salon. The establishment was a welcome change to most of the villagers, especially the wives, whose husbands had enjoyed an exclusive majority of pubs and smoke shops for far too long.

As eager as she was to stage the Vedic hymns, Martha had to acknowledge Rebecca's point of view. Old habits and animosities among the louder patriots of Hedge End were proving as hard to sweep away as winter slush. Even little Malcolm, during her last visit to Paul's, had innocently asked her what a "wog" was, after having heard the term being bandied about by some of the older boys. His grandmother had told him, after a moment's reflection, that a wog was any man who called another man a wog and simply left it at that.

"Well," Martha now withdrew an inch, "I suppose you're right, but only to a point. Wouldn't now be the best time of all to address the issue? I'd certainly never want to use his death to win anyone over, yet such martyrdom can only put a more human face on the whole affair, don't you think? I know there's still a great deal of bitterness about," she granted, recalling the poisonous debate in her son's shop, "but that only means we're all in need of a great deal of forbearance. We haven't lost India. We've restored it to its rightful owners. No matter how much help we may have given them, and how many improvements we may have made, the land was always theirs. No true Briton could ever deny the justice of that."

"If you say so, Martha," Rebecca replied with an audible

click of her hairpins, though she seemed somehow put out. "Which of these hymns, then, were you thinking of recommending we use?"

As the two friends bent together over the musical score, people came and went around them, mostly women, carrying in masses of cold air to be warmed over cups of tea and long talks. Emily Quinn was everywhere at once, refusing to let even one of her daughters deprive her of the command that she felt to be rightfully hers. "Sunlight or shade?" she would quiz each new arrival with a lemon pucker and then steer them off by the rudder of an elbow. The question was a matter of form mostly, for the entire shop shone with the radiance of painted china and freshly applied makeup.

When the time came for Martha and Rebecca to settle their bill, the latter looked up from her handbag and asked, "So how do you think Samuel will react to our using the church for this?"

"You know religion has never meant all that much to him," Martha reminded her, "ever since the two wars and the time we lost Walter. He rarely even comes with me anymore on a Sunday."

"Then perhaps it's this Gandhi connection that's put him in a paddy. That foolish jealousy of his and all. Constable Pratt said something to me this morning about his suddenly going off on his own. Is there something worse wrong that you're not telling me about, Martha?" Rebecca bore down upon her friend. "You always can, you know. Tell me any and everything that's happening in your life."

They walked outside into the steely air and turned down the street toward the Olympia. Martha hesitated for a few strides, but then she finally decided to unburden herself to her old friend — in part.

"The fact of the matter is, Rebecca, I don't know where

Samuel's at, and now I've gone and urged Constable Pratt to start the whole village and countryside looking out for him. Samuel's terribly angry with me," she said reluctantly, "and I'm still not sure I know why. Though I do have my suspicions."

"Which are?"

Clearing her throat and sniffling, Martha admitted at last that her first meeting with Gandhi in Portsmouth hadn't been her only or last contact with him and that now Samuel might have learned more about it than she would have liked.

"Really?" Rebecca breathed. "Oh, tell me, tell me! How much more was there? How long did your relationship with the master go on, then?"

"Well, all the way up until the end, actually. That's what I thought his son's letter was before I opened it, his last, posthumous message to me." With a brusque fluffing of her lapels up around her neck, Martha went on a bit more guardedly, "But you have to understand, Rebecca, that it was more of a simple friendship than a relationship. It was always perfectly innocent, perfectly honorable, more of a sister-and-brother arrangement than anything else. We kept in touch monthly by post and once in a great while by telegram, sharing our families' joys and troubles, exchanging political news, discussing religions and philosophies and even diets, and generally just the kind of small talk that longtime friends always like to share. I know now that I should have told Samuel about it — and you, too, of course — but by then Gandhi had become so famous that I was afraid it would seem immodest of me, and anyway I never felt any shame or guilt over it. To me, it was only one portion of my life that I preferred keeping to myself, a private companionship that let me say things and talk about things that I never would have with Samuel or with anyone else around here.

Not even with you, my dear," Martha concluded, "though I suppose you'll never forgive me for it now."

"Nonsense. Don't give it another thought." Rebecca Pye seemed to hold her hurt feelings in check and said, "But you must have met up with him, too, during one of his half dozen or so visits to England, didn't you? Can't you tell me a little more about those?"

Instead of answering her, Martha began berating herself for getting her friends and her neighbors involved in what was strictly a family matter between her and Samuel. "You know how much I hate wearying anyone else with my problems," she said to change the subject, once and for all. "It's such an unfair imposition on everyone and never does any of us much good in the end. Though I could use a little of your company in the house, especially at night."

"Of course, of course. I'll arrange it at once. You'd be surprised," Rebecca told her as they reached the bookshop, "at how much help other people, even total strangers, can be when you really need them."

This prediction was confirmed the following day when, to her utter amazement, Martha received an invitation to the bungalow of Rival Cobb. Samuel's whereabouts were still unknown, and her nights alone were growing steadily longer with staring and tossing. But the pleated note that the scruffy boy brought to her door promised all the resources at the journalist's disposal, so she wrapped herself in her best raglan coat and hurried to the other end of the village to see him.

Constable Pratt, it appeared, had enlisted Cobb as his first line of investigation, relying upon the widower's unofficial network of informants to broaden his search and, at the same time, not distract the boot maker himself too long from his toast. By now, Cobb had already begun his work, though so far all the responses had been in the negative.

That, in itself, was hopeful — and not. Accident or collapse was becoming less and less probable, but that left only willful, heartless abandonment.

"Old man's done a flit on you, eh?" the journalist called out to Martha when she was still fifty feet from his door. "No idea where he might have gone to ground? Well, we'll fix that soon enough, not to worry. But do come in."

The inside of Cobb's cottage met most of his visitor's expectations. Shelves and bureaus held thousands of books that seemed to be trying to topple one another onto the floor. Scraps of paper lay on all sides, and unwinding typewriter ribbons threatened to smudge any fingers that strayed too near them. Yet there were also more refined touches, a legacy perhaps from his late wife, who was said to have been a painter of some kind. Watts prints adorned the less visible walls, and black cloisonné boxes and art pewter stood in a pedestal cupboard of fumed oak. And through a back window framed by hanging secateurs and wicker trugs clotted with humus could be seen the furrows of a garden that, in season, would no doubt produce enough angelica and parsley to offset the indoor aromas of leather and cigars.

Cobb offered his guest a drop of whiskey — "against the cold," he said — but Martha would take only a cup of the coffee she smelled coming from the kitchen. Then she sat down opposite him and apologized for allowing Constable Pratt to pester him over such trivialities.

"Can't hear a word you say!" he lied cheerily with one hand behind an ear. "All I know is that the shoemaker comes to me with an assignment, and I send out a few carefully worded questionnaires to certain people who know how to keep their eyes open, and then I find out what I find out. Unhappily, at this point that's still precious little, though I trust this evening will see some small return on our efforts."

"Still," Martha objected, "it's terribly kind of you to bother for people you hardly even know."

"Hardly even know? But I first met your man back in his ironmongering days, and since then we've all come together regularly, haven't we, at our Saturday night clubs? Besides," he went on, a memory softening his features, "I understand what it is to lose the better part of oneself. My sweet Abigail passed on the sixteenth of October 1933 at nine-twenty-two on a bright Monday morning, sitting at that table right behind you, after fifty-three years, eight months, and a week and a half of blissful marriage. Must have felt right," the old man sighed gently, "when you think of it, her going in the autumn like that, with the lovely colors of decay all around her. I only hope to do the same myself when my time comes, if it ever does."

Martha politely sighed and pointed out that, in this case, her husband was merely missing temporarily.

"Quite right. Never lose hope. Isn't that, after all, what we're about, we husbands and wives?" he observed with a steadier smile. "Always either looking for or looking after each other our whole lives through?"

They talked for a while over coffee and biscuits about marriage and loss and growing old. Martha discovered that Rival Cobb had a number of astute, well-considered things to say about love and all its changes. Why was it, he wondered, that too often the world dismissed the entanglements of the heart among the elderly? Why should gray hairs be thought immune to the same kind of romantic perturbations that afflict the young? If anything, age must accentuate the effects, both good and bad. "Do you know, there are some in this very village," he said with a grave shake of his head, "who would die for love — die! — and that in their eightieth or their ninetieth year?" Present company, he hastened to assure Martha, was excluded, but the gist of it was the same. There was no putting a clock or a calendar on desire. One should never imagine that it was too late in life to be happy.

Later, on their way to the door, the journalist mentioned in a lighter tone, "I hear that you mean to offer us Hedge Enders some musical program memorializing Gandhi. Is that true?"

Rebecca Pye, Martha reflected, was encyclopedic in her gossiping.

"Only a short one," she answered cautiously. "And only as a mark of respect for a fallen man of peace."

"No, no," the widower declared in a sudden passion. "I think it's fitting, most fitting. We all need to be reminded of how Gandhi showed us that we haven't always lived up to our better selves. 'Between the idea and the reality falls the Shadow,' don't you see?" he startled her by quoting Eliot. "He was a living mirror for Britain, holding up the image of what we were in the face of what we pretended to be. And if your program can honor that, if only for an evening, then I say carry on, and damn all what any of your neighbors have to say.

"It's just that," Cobb added, his block profile coloring slightly, "I wouldn't mind sitting in on the performance myself, if you think you might be able to make some room for me."

"Oh? Do you play?"

"In my youth. The double bass. I used to acquit myself very well, though," he claimed with a comical sawing motion of his right arm across his chest, "in the Schubert *Trout* and in some of Bottesini's Elegies. I chose that particular instrument, you understand, not for its size or sound, but for its comparative anonymity. Yes, I always aspired to playing as little as possible, no more than a single note or chord per piece, if I could get away with it. Perhaps that's why I keep myself so busy now, not only to bear the absence of my Abigail, but also to atone for such habits of chronic indolence.

"And who's to say," he suggested, as he handed her down to the front walk, "that's not what your Samuel's doing, too, only taking a brief holiday from his ordinary round? At any rate, I'm confident that I shall have some good news to relay to you before another twenty-four hours have passed. Now off you go, and try not to worry too much."

But that night Martha did worry, did fret and blame herself as she tried in vain to fall asleep. Without Samuel beside her, the house came alive with sounds, wooden voices, shadows that lengthened along walls, and curtains that swung across a fleeing mouse's back, but there was no mouse. Now Martha wished that she'd taken Rebecca completely into her confidence, either today or years ago. Was it guilt that had held her back? Strange, but never before now had Martha felt that emotion in relation to her friendship with Gandhi. The Indian had always seemed so well mannered and refined, and as time went on his physical presence had grown more and more attenuated, until he'd become little more than pure spirit. How could even Samuel ever have objected to his wife's communing with someone who was so much more than a mere man and, therefore, in a way so much less? In fact, as she grew drowsier, Martha was sure that her husband would never have objected — yet that hardly justified her, did it, in keeping the secret from him for so long and finally leaving him to discover it for himself like some criminal past?

The next morning, Sunday, Rival Cobb proved true to his word. Then appeared the same shabby boy with a second note. This one was even more laconic than the last.

"Spent much time lately," it read, "with dear old Uncle Oliver?"

Martha folded the paper into a tiny square and held it tightly between her palms. Oliver, of course, was Samuel's lunatic half brother who still refused to leave his hut on the outskirts of Imber. If that was, indeed, where her husband had chosen to hide himself, she began to fear that she might never win him back.

6

IN PAUL'S OLD, CRIPPLED MORRIS, with the usual winter obstacles and the rebuilding state of the roads, the drive up to the northwestern quarter of Salisbury Plain took the greater part of a morning. Delays and detours were to be expected, the damage wrought by years of military traffic appearing around almost every corner. The weather was accommodating enough. Overnight, arctic air had moved down from the north to displace the shaggy clouds, and the day had dawned blue with cold and clear. Except for the freezing temperature, one might have thought that a midwinter spring had arrived, the way the chalk ranges opened out into limitless vistas and the hibernating barley and turnip fields blossomed with damp, black stalks. Solitary habitations of cob walls cropped up on ridges like mushrooms, leading the eye eventually to unknown or barely remembered villages where the clay-smeared twigs of wattle and daub predominated and cowlick tufts of thatch nodded beneath winds. A rough-hewn Monday industriousness greeted the travelers at every turn until they knew the sneaking pleasure that the sick and the malingering feel whenever they play truant from their day-to-day lives.

Against the dictates of her conscience, Martha rather enjoyed the outing. Leaving Hedge End behind, with all its claustrophobic memories and duties, gave her the chance to take a deep breath again. The bouncing of the country lanes combined with the height of the sky, almost white in its purity, to rattle her out of the darker mood into which the events of the past week had led her. She had, moreover, missed her son's company of late. Her weekly visits to his home were often adulterated by the dour presence of his wife, and even the grandchildren sometimes flustered her with their animation. But today Martha and Paul had each other all to themselves.

As a man, Paul could be seen accurately reflected in the car they were riding in now. Breezy, makeshift, with a dinner-plate-sized hole in the passenger's floor through which twinkled the racing macadam, the Minor was one of the few bequests that Paul had agreed to accept from his father. Unlike his two sisters, Paul had always been composed and quiet, satisfied with so little in life that his parents often worried about his future. His ambitions were few — to work honorably, to surround himself with family, to make friends. As a child, he might have been found staring for hours on end at a blank wall. And, when asked what he was looking at, he would reply, "All of it." Sensing the world in its molecular entirety seemed of the utmost importance to him, and he would rise at five in the morning to arrange every bottle, brush, and towel in his shop. Similarly, as a recruiter during the war, Paul had visited the homes of soldiers he'd helped send on their way, "only," as he said, "to finish my duty to them." Such scrupulous attention to detail mystified Martha, who, as a teacher of children, had always been blithely content with chaos, but she put it down to Samuel and his shop in Bursledon Road and its alphabetical order. That, too, Paul must have inherited from his father.

This single-mindedness in her son perhaps explained his unquestioning acceptance of his role today as a go-between for his estranged parents. When he had driven over to Hedge End to collect Martha, he hadn't even asked the purpose of their journey. And now, more than halfway to Imber, it was his mother who felt that she had to excuse her stealing him away from his home and his business for the day.

"It seems," she began, "that your father got it into his head to visit Uncle Oliver last week and —"

"Well, I'm glad someone has," Paul interjected. "I haven't in a month."

Martha turned toward her son. "You drive up to see him? How long has this been going on?"

"Oh, for quite some time now. The poor old man has no one else, and now that they've taken away his village I fear for his mind." Paul reached for a lower gear and rounded a deserted cruck cottage screened by a stand of pollard willows. "I can't imagine how he keeps body and soul together in that windy shack of his," he continued. "I've tried to take him some food and clothing now and again, and I even offered to hammer up some shingles to cover the more open spots in the roof and walls. But he wouldn't hear of it. He's even more proud and stubborn than Father, if that's possible."

"Is he well, then?" Martha asked. "Is he — himself?"

"As much, I suppose, as he ever was. You know Uncle Oliver. No wife, no family, and now no real home to speak of. He was never a very strong man, but in the last five years he's fallen even lower. I tell you, it's scandalous how the army turned the whole village out, man, woman, and child, just so they could have somewhere to practice their urban war games. Did you hear that their local blacksmith died of a broken heart after his favorite bellows somehow vanished? It put me in mind of Grandfather Weekes, that did, and I wondered how we should have reacted had he been so unjustly run off his smithy up in Droxford."

As Paul reviewed Imber's late misfortunes, the transformations around the village began to materialize before them. On either side of the lane, the remains of prefabricated Anderson air-raid shelters gradually gave way to newer Nissen tunnel huts that announced a continuing military presence. In this part of the Wylye Valley, mullioned windows, flintwork, and lath and plaster still held sway, especially among the older buildings. But the closer they came to Uncle Oliver's, the more cement and corrugated iron they began to see. Assemblages of black-green or gray metal suddenly sprouted up behind natural ricks, and lonely cans of gasoline stood enigmatically at set intervals, as if in a parade relay. At the same time, mile by mile, the hard winter carapace of Salisbury Plain became even bleaker and less human. The silhouettes of stalking automatons might sometimes be seen guarding the horizon, while nearer to the road camouflaged barbed wire bound straggling vines and hedgerows. From the last hill above Imber, the village appeared deceptively tranquil, almost asleep, the skeleton of the parish church watching over the concrete façades that were being erected to replace the native cottages of timber and brick. But on roofs and inside doorways, patrolling rifle barrels and helmets seemed to have transported an acre of wartime France into the very heart of England.

It was only in these final moments before their arrival that Martha allowed herself to think about the coming reunion with Samuel. They'd been apart for just a few days, yet the distance of this separation felt different to her from any earlier ones. After so many years, she could no longer recall much about their courtship, the flutterings before mirrors and the anxious search for words that must have possessed her at twenty-two. But she was sure it had been an awkward, stumbling time, and now some vestige of that aching self-consciousness had returned to fluster her old age. She didn't think it fair, having to plead with her own husband for nothing more than their usual serenity. She resented his thoughtlessness and inwardly vowed not to give in to any of his mulish demands or his fears of being unloved. Still, all the while, she couldn't help thinking that she was probably even more to blame for this situation than he.

Quite a bit more than probably, Martha had to confess to herself as she and her son drove the last few miles in silence. For it wasn't entirely true, what she'd told Rebecca after their recent lunch together at the Eglantine. Martha and Gandhi had indeed always maintained a perfectly platonic friendship between them, yes, but over time there had also been some degree of romance that had, against all their best efforts to the contrary, risen to the surface. It had never been anything blatant or wanton, nothing that most husbands would even notice. But Martha could still remember the gradually accumulating "dears" and "hearts" in their correspondence, as well as the "loves" and "all my loves" that started to appear above both of their signatures as if by accident. She felt sorry for those endearments now, though at the moment of their use they had sounded chaste enough. Her sense of guilt, it seemed, was growing larger with every day that passed since Gandhi's death, and she found herself wondering why now and why not before. Perhaps the answer lay in their letters. All of his to her had been destroyed as soon as they'd been read in dark buses or far out in the back yard, but hers to him must still be in existence somewhere. If Samuel ever got hold of those, Martha frankly didn't know how she could ever defend herself.

As soon as Paul turned down the rutted drive leading into Uncle Oliver's property, he nodded ahead, and remarked, "Look, Mother. I expect you might see the same sight on any farm in the land. What do you think?"

Martha followed his gaze. "What is it?"

"Only two men, staring down at a patch of grass. They might be talking about planting," he speculated, "or discovering a lost gear or waiting for a rabbit to show its head. But anyone seeing them would think they'd been standing there forever."

At one corner of the yard, just where a rusted plow lay nestled in weeds, the two half brothers were in profile, their matching angled chins and backs bent forward as though made of ruined masonry. They were so engrossed in whatever they were discussing that the visitors were almost upon them before they noticed.

"What's ailing your foot?" Samuel asked his wife as soon as he saw her.

"Nothing," she answered, though secretly she was pleased that he was speaking to her again. The fact was that a blade of pain had started up in her right instep when she got out of the car, effectively hobbling her, and it would continue until she reached home again.

But what surprised them both was how shy they suddenly felt around each other, shy and clumsy. Even after having been married for nearly a lifetime, they could still blush as though they were approaching their first formal dance together.

"It's the army!" declared Oliver, who lived on the perimeter of the mock battlefield. "They've put something in the water."

"Oliver," Martha greeted him.

The rheumy eyes squinted across at her. "Mother?"

"No, Oliver," Samuel said, taking his arm and leading him toward the house. "It's only Martha. She's come with our son on a short visit. Have we anything warm to serve them?"

The interior of the farmhouse was little better than the exterior. Whereas the outside stood in a collapsed stack of wood and lime-washed bricks, the inside was shrunken with too much furniture, curling linoleum, and the close, twiggy fragrance of dust. The chairs and tables and sofas of a lifetime's pointless collecting seemed to lie about in as random a state as Oliver himself, with his belt hanging off one hip and his unshaven bewilderment. While he set about preparing first cold tea, then warm milk without tea, then hot tea overwhelmed by milk gone bad, Martha took stock of her surroundings and tried to remember how often she had been here before. Not often, she finally decided. It was not that she felt any direct hostility toward her husband's family. She'd got on well enough with his parents before their deaths and had once or twice welcomed into her home some distant cousins from the Cotswolds. But even with her own relations she had maintained only the most tenuous of ties. Her sister in Avebury had died a dozen years ago, while the brother who had emigrated before the Great War to Perth — "furthest from anywhere," as he put it — was now no more than a photographed memory, though he did write her annually with an offer to pay her way over for a visit. As Martha sat alone in a sprung armchair, holding an empty saucer before her, she felt with a soft jolt how isolated she and Samuel had let themselves become in Hedge End. This circumstance couldn't have been by design, for neither of them had any reason to thrust their respective families aside. But over the years, the edifice of their marriage must have gradually become a walled city unto itself, one which was almost too self-sufficient to need any outside contacts whatsoever.

Once Oliver had succeeded in serving the tea to his own satisfaction, he dove into an adjoining room, and his three guests held their collective breath. It was widely known that the old man had neither opened nor discarded any gift he'd ever been given and that the second bedroom was a storehouse of moldering packages and ventilated boxes that used to move, but now lay still. When he came out again, he was unwrapping a ribboned case of what might have been soaps, but turned out to be gourmet cakes from some forgotten era.

"Could you taste this," he said eagerly to Martha, offering her one, "and tell me if it's all right?"

She took the cake with a brave smile. "I'm sure it's fine."

"I'll have two," said Samuel defiantly.

"They must be delicious," Oliver assured them. "I was given them by a delightful Cornish lady who was quite taken with me and used to make the most delicious tiddy oggy pasties. She wasn't English, you know, not really. But I think I loved her, at least as much as any man can love any woman. Nothing came of it, as I recall." He sighed as he sat down and spilled tea on his misbuttoned vest. "But I thanked God for that in the end. The children we'd have had, oh, they would have been the most hideous creatures, so flat and thin and lacking in depth. She was that way, too, so much so that I'd lose sight of her whenever she swung sideways to me. Why, the boys would have been poles and the girls mere switches! And you can't have cardboard children like that, can you," he asked, looking at each of them in turn, "running around the playgrounds and down the school hallways, no matter how much you dote upon them and want to keep them? No, no, it simply wouldn't have done!"

The others in the room hummed in practiced assent. As a young man, Oliver had been kicked in the head by his favorite horse and had never been the same since. No one knew whether it was the blow or the betrayal that had wounded him more, but since then he'd been unable to distinguish a third dimension and lived in a universe of cruel surfaces. Changes in position confused him as well, so that stray sheep would suddenly appear at his side and saucepans from the stove would become platters as soon as they were transferred to the table. Long ago, a specialist had stopped by and pronounced him brain-damaged, but since the condition hadn't seemed to hamper his farming, nothing had been done. In a way, the family had derived some comfort from the diagnosis. Now they could blame all of Uncle Oliver's eccentricities on his clinical agnosia and none on a suspect bloodline.

"Well," Samuel ruminated over his pair of cakes, his late reticence now gone, "I rather think you're well out of it, Oliver, with the Cornish and all. Bringing a woman like that into your home would have been like bringing in a foreigner. And everyone knows what a hazard that can be."

"Still," Martha put in, "it might have been better than his continuing to live on here alone."

"Or worse."

"Not to mention the cooking she could have done for him."

Uncle Oliver turned from one of them to the other. "There is that."

"And the cleaning," she added with a shudder at the room.

"Oh," the farmer shook his head, "but I shouldn't have

wanted anyone to disturb anything. Not after the enormous effort it's cost me to put the place just so."

And he surveyed his tottering pillars of newspapers and overloaded cabinets as lovingly as a carpenter might have gazed at his workbench.

"Father's right, though," said Paul after a moment. "Sometimes marriage isn't all it's made out to be, is it? There's often such a gulf between people, even after years and years of being together, that one wonders if the time and sacrifice have been worth it. If a person is only going to feel lonely anyway —" Paul broke off, finally realizing what he was saying and who was listening. Then he concluded weakly, "Of course, that's not true for the majority of couples, I suppose."

A heavy silence filled the room, until Oliver asked his guests, "Have you ever noticed how you can walk out into the road, look both ways as you've been taught, and see nothing but a single motorcar perhaps, miles off, no more than a mote? Then, just as you're about to cross, you find it roaring down upon you like a winter storm — lorries have done this — and it's all you can do to leap back into the safety of the bramble bushes. Do the rest of you," he inquired in an academic tone, "find it necessary to plan every moment of your day as carefully as I do?"

"I still say," Samuel repeated as he brushed the crumbs off his lap, "that a man my brother's age can't afford to let himself be bullied into anything that might do him more harm than good. Tie him to a strange woman at this late period in his life, and what has he got?"

"Company?" interrupted Martha.

"Heartache," her husband said darkly, his eyes trained on an empty space midway between his wife and son. "Nothing but misunderstandings and disappointments and constantly being surprised by people he thought he knew. I wouldn't wish that on anyone, least of all my own kin."

Martha nearly stopped breathing, then composed herself. "Even so, he might welcome the change." Martha turned toward Oliver and asked in a raised voice, "Wouldn't you relish a bit of novelty, dear, to brighten your day?"

"I could do with a new set of gnashers," he proposed, clacking his worn dentures in his mouth as he thoughtfully stirred his tea with a finger. "As it is now, proper food's gone beyond me."

Samuel laughed out loud. "Well, there you have it!" he exclaimed. "What Oliver needs is a dentist, not a wife. Whatever you do, don't saddle him with someone he might spend the rest of his life with, only to discover at the end that most of it's been a lie. Is there anything worse than misplaced trust?"

"I wasn't aware, Samuel, that marriage meant no more to you than that. If I'd known this fifty years ago —"

"Perhaps you ought to have asked."

"Asked? Asked whom, I should like to know?"

"Why not me?" he cried. "Have my opinions never counted for anything with you?"

"Don't start with me," Martha warned him, folding her hands in front of her. "You know perfectly well that I've always respected your thoughts and feelings during our life together. Can I help it if, by now, it's only natural that neither of us has much of anything new to say?"

"But all the others do, then, your fellow teachers and booksellers and correspondents, even those on the other side of the world? I know I may have been only a common shopkeeper in my time," he sniffed with the childish bitterness of the very old, "with oily hands and a library of motor journals, but that doesn't mean I didn't have a few insights of my own. A man learns a lot about life and people, working at the same trade for so long, even in a place as small as Hedge End."

"As he does in farming," Oliver agreed, "though I've never tried it myself."

Momentarily perplexed by the sudden hurt in her husband's voice, Martha looked about her for aid, until Paul said, "No one that I know of, Father, has ever belittled your choice of profession. Surely never Mother nor I."

"Then why was it," Samuel wanted to know, "that she felt she needed to search so far outside her own home for friendship?"

"Friendship?" his wife stammered, and their son helplessly lifted his palms between them.

Samuel's mouth drew down into a pout as he finished quietly. "I'd always thought that's what husbands and wives were meant to be to each other. The first, last, and best of friends. Was I so wrong?"

"No," Martha answered in a voice that was almost too low to hear. "But neither was I."

Now, finally sensing that his father somehow knew as much of the truth as he did, Paul rose abruptly to his feet and said to the farmer beside him, "Fancy a breath of fresh air, Uncle Oliver? Why not come out and show me that well you say keeps silting over?" Then he left his parents alone and facing each other in the sitting room's mustiness and clutter.

Martha allowed a lengthy silence to pass, during which time the earth continued to turn and the house to settle around them, before she spoke to her husband again.

"What is it exactly, Samuel," she began, "that you'd like us to talk about?"

He hesitated, then replied, "Well, correct me if I'm mistaken, but as near as I can figure it, you and I have been to the Isle of Wight no more than three times — first right after our wedding, then later with the children, and lastly with

Nellie's children. Yet not once," he said very deliberately, "did we ever have occasion to stay at Shelton's Vegetarian Hotel, 25 Madeira Road, Ventnor."

Martha couldn't help smiling to herself at his investigative skills, so much like those in the detective stories that he used to read before his vision grew too weak for anything but illustrations of spanners and pins. Then she assumed a demeanor as serious as his own.

"Ah, the ceramic plate from the lower left-hand drawer of the sideboard." She nodded in recollection. "I'd forgotten about it altogether. I can't think how you found it or, once you did, how it came to have any meaning for you."

"Even a foolish old man," her husband muttered, "can put two and two together, given enough time and resources."

The Houghtons sat stiffly across from each other, alone in a room that was not theirs, the day's light fractured by the lurching of tree shadows across the window. Outside, the tread and voices of Paul and Oliver receded and surged as they wandered about the yard.

Martha and Samuel seemed reluctant to let their eyes meet. Each stared at a chair leg or a drape cord or a lamp or whorls of dust at whose nature neither dared guess, yet never fixedly and never allowing their lines of sight to cross. This made for a conversation as between complete strangers.

"I still can't believe," whispered Martha at last, "that I had such boldness at a young age to persuade poor Aunt Feemy to take me across to the island. She had all the reason in the world not to, having already embarrassed both herself and Gandhi during a rubber of bridge on that first evening. But I was a mere girl, and besides she'd never been able to deny me anything. So we sailed on the next boat and followed him to the same hotel he had told us he'd be staying at. It was all just a lark, really, an excuse for a springtime romp between a couple of gals."

"And Gandhi didn't find this a bit much?" Samuel asked with a prudishness that was unusual for him. "To be run down, I mean, by a lovesick girl and a woman whose reputation couldn't stand much scrutiny? And him a married man and a father who was supposed to be so famous for his morality?"

Ignoring the insult to her late aunt, Martha said that he had felt nothing of the kind. "We didn't even learn all the facts about his true situation until sometime later. Actually, in those days he sometimes used to pass himself off as a bachelor, as many of the other Indian boys did in order to win over companions. Otherwise, the huge differences between their arranged relationships back home and our freer English ones always left them lonely and frustrated. As for Gandhi, I think he took it as something of a compliment that he was able to pique the interest of a young Western girl. Remember," she pointed out, "he was new to this country, new to our world as a whole, and only a few years older than I was, still not much more than a child himself. I'm sure he must have been charmed by all the attention. And it's not as if either Aunt Feemy or I pestered him in any way. We passed it off as a coincidence, lunched once or twice in the same room as he, and sat in on part of his vegetarian meeting at the Friendly Society Hall. Auntie, I think, had her hands full, flirting outrageously with a retired fisherman, and I spent most of my time mooning about after my new friend. It was all as innocent as the month of May we were in, and after a day or two Gandhi took the train back to London. Alone, need I add?"

"And that's all you two did?" Samuel asked. "You didn't happen to walk the beaches and the limestone hills together?

I know you were always mad for strolling in your younger years."

"We might have. I don't know if I can really say after all this time. Haven't you ever noticed," she asked him, sitting forward, "how all our earlier experiences seemed to have happened to other people? They were we, of course, as we are they, I'm not disputing that. But, now that we have so much of our lives behind us, don't you sometimes feel that all those things we did when we were young were done by someone else, only using our names? We have so many memories." Martha groaned with a shake of the head. "And, as lovely as most of them are, and as much as I wouldn't trade away even one of them for anything, there are times when the sheer hoarding of them gets to be too much for me. Particularly in the quiet of the night, or when I'm sitting alone over my sewing, I ask myself if it might not be better to be like Mother was in her final months, not remembering anything."

Fidgeting in his chair, Samuel quickly grew impatient with his wife's airy philosophizing. There were certain specific matters between them that needed to be addressed, and he was not about to be put off the program that he'd spent most of the past week laying out. "There was never any mention, then, of your running off to London with him or even all the way to India?"

"Oh, good Lord, no!" scoffed Martha. Then she said, "As you mentioned, he was already married with a child. And he was always so busy with his studies and his duties and wondering who he was going to be and what he was going to do with his life that he couldn't have had many spare moments for me. Anyway, what could a mere slip of a girl from Droxford have had to offer a man of the world like him?"

"What every girl has to offer every man," Samuel answered gruffly. "Her innocence."

Martha recoiled. "Don't talk nonsense, especially concerning things you know so little about. As a matter of fact," she continued with just a hint of disappointment, "he'd been struggling with that very subject even before coming here. It seems his father had passed away on the same night that he and his young wife were — well, you know. And, afterward, he took to blaming himself for failing his father in his last moments, as well as for the early death of the baby that came just after. It always seemed so sad to me that he should have taken so much guilt upon himself only for acting normally, but it appears that was a large part of his character. He was forever intent," she marveled, "on making such a great, loud fuss over simply being good. That was one thing in him that I could never fully understand."

If her husband had been slightly more observant, or if his concentration hadn't been disturbed by the sight of Oliver flailing at branches for buds of crusted snow, he would have seen a shadow of yearning cross his wife's face. But, as it was, by the time he'd turned back she was her old self again.

"So," Martha resumed, "now you can see that we were only a pair of silly children from two widely separate societies who became friends at one special time and place, as I told you before. And there was never really anything more to it than that."

In a voice as low as if he were waking an infant, Samuel reminded her, "Yet that childhood friendship didn't end then and there, did it? Not quite."

His wife sat very still, as if to move would be to commit an irrevocable act, studying the new confidence in him. "No," she finally said in resignation. "No, it didn't. And now I expect you'll want to hear everything."

"I think I'm entitled to, don't you?"

Martha nodded, looked about wearily, exhaled, and went on, "Well, there were only five visits in all that Gandhi made to England over the years. Do you really want the dates? Let me see, there was the first to Portsmouth, of course, in 'ninety-one, when I was sixteen and he was twenty-two. The next wasn't until some fifteen years later, when he stayed at the Cecil in London. That's where the address book came from that you probably found at the bottom of my cedar chest."

"As I recall," Samuel put in, "wasn't that the time you were supposed to have gone into the city to meet your sister and came back feeling so unwell that eventually our Walter didn't survive his first months? Was Sally even up from Avebury then, I'm beginning to wonder now?"

Without responding directly, Martha noted that Gandhi's third visit to England had coincided with Paul's birth in 1909. "He was the only one of our children not to be born in Hedge End, you'll remember. What had happened was," she explained as calmly as she could, "that Gandhi had written to invite me to a meeting of the West London Ethical Society in a church at 45 Queens Road, Bayswater."

"Ah, the ticket in the Tolstoy volume from the box of books out in the shed," Samuel pointed out.

"Yes, that's right."

"And," he added in a more sinister tone, "the dying uncle whom you told me you just had to minister to alone. What was his name again?"

Martha swallowed hard. "If you're going to bring up every single one of my little white lies, we're never going to finish with all this before nightfall."

Samuel bowed his head in mock surrender and let her go on.

"The fourth visit wasn't really a visit at all," Martha said more hurriedly now, the daylight beginning to wane in the room around them. "In nineteen-fourteen, you were over in Flanders and I'd gone to help out at Netley Hospital, where I got that silver spoon that I gave to Paul. Gandhi had organized a medical Indian Volunteer Corps, and eventually they were assigned to our hospital. But they never let him come along, for they saw him as a troublemaker in the military, and I had to visit him for only a day or two in London. By then," she reminisced with a blank gaze at the ceiling, "he was in his mid-forties, but he still looked like a youngster who was trying to pretend to be one of us and not who he truly was. He'd just come up from South Africa in a dress suit and a fluff of thick hair and a mustache, and even though he talked about committing his life to poverty and service, he struck me as being slightly false, off a note or two. I upbraided him terribly for holding his welcoming reception at the Cecil and for living in the fancy house of a diamond merchant friend of his in Talbot Road, so much so that he finally retreated to a humble hostel near the Earl's Court train station. I like to think," Martha said, smiling, "that I was some small help in steering him down a path that was more in keeping with his life's true goals."

"And the fifth and final visit?" Samuel sighed, sounding more anxious than she must have been to finish. "The sheet music from Chichester?"

His wife paused to gather her thoughts. "The bishop, Dr. George Bell, was a friend of his," she said, "and Gandhi stopped by for only a few days. When I met him there, while you and Alice were out shopping, I was shocked at the change that had taken place in him over the past seventeen years. He was so much thinner than before, pulled almost transparent like taffy, starved and deliberately poor and ethereal in his white robes and with his voice so quiet that everyone had to lean forward to hear him. I nearly didn't recognize my old friend, even though I'd seen the same photographs of him in the newspapers that we'd all seen. His attitude was different toward me, too, more casual and intimate, almost as if we were some long-divorced couple who had met by chance in a mutual friend's library. Before, during his previous visit, when I was still an impressionable woman of thirty-nine, I have to admit that there was a bit of an electrical charge between us that probably came more from my missing you so much, Samuel, than from anything else. But," Martha quickly added, "there were never, ever any intimacies offered or accepted at any time, no more than a firm handshake and a loose embrace. At that time, you see, Gandhi was a full eight years into his *brahmacharya* vow of complete chastity, even in his marriage, and I, naturally, would never have dreamt of being unfaithful to you. Then, during his last visit, the two of us seemed more like a pair of stodgy, worn-out dowagers who had no more energy for anything but to compare our wrinkles and wish that our children hadn't grown up so fast and so far away from us. We must have made a sad sight," she concluded mournfully, "standing there side by side, contemplating the long, separate lives we'd passed together, and complaining about how sixty years of age would probably mark the last time we would ever see one another alive. And, as it turned out, it was."

Martha looked up as Samuel slowly pulled himself to his feet and began pacing the room as well as his stiff legs and Oliver's tumbledown furniture would let him. He glanced out the window at his half brother, who was snagged on a stile, he turned over papers and fabrics whose soot smudged his fingers, and he moved his hands on and off his hips as if he were performing some arcane brand of calisthenics. Then he came to a halt just between her and the window, right where he knew his shadow would loom impressively over her.

"I'm curious," he said more lightly. "What did you call

him when you were together or in your letters? Gandhi, as you do now? Mahatma? What?"

"I called him Mohandas, his given name."

"No nicknames? No pet names?"

"I think not. Why?" asked Martha. "What are you getting at?"

"And his wife. What's her name?"

"Was. She died four years ago. Kasturbai."

Now both Martha and Samuel were frowning at each other, though for different reasons.

"And what was she like, do you know?" he persisted, retreating to his chair again. "Did you ever meet her?"

"Yes," Martha said. "As a matter of fact, I did, very briefly. During the 1914 visit."

Samuel was about to react to this information, but after considering for a moment only repeated, "So what was she like? Wait, don't tell me. Let me guess. Was she fiercely independent and intent upon working at her own career, such as teaching? Did she dally with the suffragette movement at any time, read forbidden authors, and arrange religious programs that flew in the face of local sentiments? Was she strong in body and mind, did she travel alone, was she unconcerned with keeping a strict house, and did she obey her husband only in those things that to her mind deserved to be obeyed? Do you think, Martha, that any of this would accurately describe her?"

"No," his wife murmured. "No, I don't."

"And Gandhi himself," Samuel proceeded. "Would you say that he was the kind of man who preferred motor journals over religious texts or a hearty meal over fasting? Do you think he would rather have spent a night at a pub with his mates or at a temple alone in prayer? Was he ever satisfied with creating and preserving one good, healthy family, or was he more concerned with saving the whole world, the effects on his own family be damned? What do you think about that, my dear? You knew him. Was that the kind of man he was?"

With a shake of her head from side to side, Martha asked her husband what he was trying to prove with such absurd characterizations.

"Only that we all tend to look to others for what we miss in those we already know. Gandhi found you fascinating," Samuel conceded unwillingly, "because you represented all the freedom and strength that he missed in his own wife without realizing it. And you were drawn to him because you know that I've never been the kind of fellow to keep up with your reading and your spiritual musings. That's also why neither of you probably ever told the truth to your spouses. Unconsciously, as Dr. Little would say, you were afraid of hearing the same sort of things that I've just told you, because then you would both have had to admit to yourselves what you couldn't stand to contemplate. That you two really were in love."

"But we weren't!" Martha objected loudly enough to bring Paul and Oliver closer to the window as if to urge them on. "We wrote and talked and walked and shared our thoughts and hopes and fears together and relaxed in each other's company. But we were never lovers or in love."

"Don't you see, Martha?" Samuel said in a surprisingly gentle voice. "The writing, the talking and the walking, and the relaxed sharing of your hopes and fears — all those things *are* love. I thought you knew that already."

And then the woman across from him sat still and smiled, as if after so many decades of the same old certainties she had finally discovered something totally new.

The drive back to Hedge End felt longer and more wearisome than before. The ancient Morris wheezed at every rise, and through the hole in the floor blew a wintry chill that was moistened by the wet road. Against the windshield, the increasing snowfall defied gravity as the flakes flew toward them and then swooped up. They might have been sailing through a field of stars rather than through an earthly countryside blinded by night.

Paul waited until he thought his mother had warmed herself sufficiently before he ventured to ask, "Is Father staying on at Uncle Oliver's for a while, then?"

"For a while."

"That's good," he suggested. "That'll give him some time to calm down, and then you two can get back to your normal lives again. Father isn't as giving and forgiving as he should be, I don't think, and I'm not just saying so because of the checkered history between us. Perhaps that's why I went along with forwarding all those letters to you from India over the years. I expect I thought you deserved something more, something better out of life, than what you had, just as we all do. So did Alice and Nellie, once I let them in on the secret, too."

"You told them? When was this?"

"Right after Gandhi was killed. I thought it couldn't do any harm to our family then, as long as they didn't bother Father with it. Was I so wrong?"

"No, it's just that you children are still young, and the young are forever too ready to criticize. When you're older," she predicted, "you'll learn that it's our flaws that make us what we are and, in the end, make us even more lovely and worth forgiving. That was one area where poor Gandhi fell a bit short, I'm afraid, in his accepting imperfections in himself and in the rest of us. I can't tell you how many of his letters were taken up with the most common human shortcomings, all our little weaknesses and passions and fears. He accused himself first, and with a loving heart," she hurried to add, "but he still thought we all needed to be refined ever purer and purer, almost out of existence. Especially after he'd come to embrace a life of poverty, he seemed to forget how important it is for people to be wrong much of the time.

"I suppose," Martha concluded with a glance at the watery city lights sliding across her window, "he would have had any number of harsh things to say about Samuel, had they ever chanced to meet. But I think there, too, he would have been mistaken."

In Hedge End, Martha refused her son's help up the walk, promising only that she would ring him as early as she could tomorrow morning. She absentmindedly rummaged through the letterbox, drew out the day's post, and let herself into the sleeping house. Coming home alone was something she knew she would never get used to, but she trusted that she shouldn't have to try. Samuel, she was sure, would come back to her before the end of the week, especially once he'd tired of Oliver's ways and his dubious meals. He would soon enough begin to miss his wife's fresh scones and long-simmered stews and even her patient reminders for him to walk more and smoke less.

Martha was halfway up the stairs before she felt the coarse texture of the top letter and glimpsed the by now familiar array of foreign stamps. Then she stopped and sagged against the handrail, calculating that this second message from Bombay must have been sent just after the first. What kind of frenzy, she asked herself in the darkness of the second-floor landing, could have possessed her old friend's dying son now?

7

THE MEMORIAL CONCERT for Gandhi in St. John's Church came off far better than anyone could have expected. Beneath its single spire and behind its Swanage stone walls, nearly three hundred people sat or stood and listened conscientiously to selections from Holst's *Choral Hymns from the Rig Veda*. Everyone agreed that they'd never seen such a turnout before. From Botley and West End, and from even as far away as Wickham, mothers and fathers brought their parents and children to take part. The weather might have had something to do with the success of the recital. The night was free of clouds, obsidian in its black height and glassy stars. Over the hardened snow, the tires of the cars groaned in protest and rolled no more smoothly than octagons. Work boots crackled loudly across the shards of grass, and in the ice ladies' heels left puncture wounds that bled water. But it was the appearance of the church itself more than anything else that brought in the audience. Regal, yet austere, St. John's raised its crosses, its

Tudor windows, and its clock dials into the dark air and welcomed every passerby with a shimmer of warmth and stained-glass light that reached all the way down Church Lane.

Inside stood a line of choristers in white surplices and ruffs, along with local instrumental accompanists, lighting that had been reduced to candelabra and sconces alone, and a chair maker who was acting as the evening's conductor. Of the fourteen hymns in Holst's masterpiece, Martha had chosen five, less than half an hour of music, and those exclusively from the first, second, and fourth groups. The third called for a women's chorus and a solo harp, but the harpist had declared that she did not feel up to the task. Helen Maddick was quite accomplished for her age, but that was only fifteen, and her cheeks flamed red even at the center of the small orchestra — the heat and the closeness, she insisted. So the program commenced with a fairly simple chant to an "Unknown God" for mixed chorus and orchestra, skating dangerously close to sacrilege, then turned more boldly Hindu with odes to Agni, the god of fire, and Varuna, the god of water. The first sang of "living on in our children," and the second spoke of happier times when "broad were the heavens, long were the days." The brief show closed with a pair of funeral hymns, one for women and strings and one for men singing *a cappella* with a baritone soloist.

During the concert, Martha stood in her accustomed place at the right end of the choir. It was her hope that by participating in tonight's activities she could somehow close a chapter in her life that had been left open for too long. Yet for all her hard work and dedication to the performance, she found herself feeling less than inspired. Perhaps it was Samuel's absence that deflated her, or the fact that the memorial seemed intended more for a departed world leader than for a friend whose mannerisms she suddenly found hard to recall. So as not to arouse any latent prejudices, there were no banners hanging in the church, no posted photographs, no smoldering incense to perfume the air with holiness. Fortunately, though, most of the members of the audience seemed caught up in the occasion. The pub landlord and the greengrocer both nodded at thc rhythms, their children swaying from side to side in polite boredom, while even Mrs. Ladbrook softened enough to give the singers her grudging approval. Yet, for some reason, Martha still remained unmoved. She fretted about the constancy of her voice's timbre and she wished that she had some face other than Rebecca Pye's to turn to for encouragement. But, as for helping her bid farewell to the man who had been taken from her so violently at the end of last month, the music at first failed miserably.

Not until the choirs came to the last two hymns did she notice in herself some response. The penultimate work, a "Funeral Chant," was a round of fading and overlapping female voices with passages that might have been written specially for the moment:

> Yea unto them whose fiery zeal
> Hath burned a path to paradise,
> May he go forth!
>
> To those the heroes of the fight,
> Whose lives were given as sacrifice,
> May he go forth!

As she now began to join in more vigorously with the others, Martha could see at the edge of her vision the young harpist relishing her anonymous role among the strings and, beyond her, Rival Cobb taxing himself in the accompaniment's lowest registers. The widower's face was fixed with intensity as he expressed an entire year's practicing in a single night, and the sight of so much disinterested fervor shamed Martha into redoubling her own efforts.

In the last piece, too, the same "Hymn to Manas" that Martha had been reading through a week ago at home, she seemed to hear some new, more personal overtones. Here, she was amazed to see Constable Pratt step forward to take the solo baritone part. His singing voice proved to be as otherworldly as his hair, distant and floating, but as heartfelt as a child's. With his arms hung like stalactites at his sides, Pratt projected toward the front doors of the church a paean to the man who now lived "within the splendor of the sun." Martha, consigned with the rest of the women's chorus to silence, felt something within her melt away at the sound of the plaintive refrain. She followed the various canon lines as they wove about one another, always returning, always comforting. In the course of the song, Martha reviewed a host of memories that finally left her almost asleep on her feet, yet at peace. Even Rita Venden, where she stood with some of her BBC colleagues near the hymnal cabinet, remarked upon Mrs. Houghton's visible transformation.

On her way down from the choir platform, Martha floated through her neighbors as through a ground fog. She searched for and found Rebecca Pye, and together they hurried out ahead of the crowd into the still night. Then, on their slow walk back to Martha's house, they enjoyed one of the best half hours they'd ever had, though neither of them spoke a word.

As usual, the telephone connection between Hedge End and Chichester was not the best, and Martha had to strain forward in her chair to hear her daughter's voice. Alice's words came across the distance as if before a gale, or as though in a tunnel with echoing limestone walls.

"But Father's well enough, you say?" Alice asked again. "Only in a temporary funk over this whole Gandhi situation, I take it?"

"As far as I can tell," Martha promised. "You know your father. Once he gets some notion into his head, it's there to stay, no matter how petty it may be."

"Or not."

"Pardon?"

Unreal voices seemed to come between them, so that Martha wondered whom she was speaking to.

"I said," Alice repeated more loudly, "I thought there might be something more to it than you're allowing. I don't know how I should feel, if someone I loved had —"

"But you've no basis for comparison, do you, dear? Being single, I mean."

"Still."

To make amends, Martha went on, "Of course, you're probably right. I have behaved like a beast, no doubt, and if I had it to do over again, well, I dare say I'd do things differently or not at all. But these are insights that none of us ever has until it's too late, do we, and the best we can do is to try to repair the damage that's already been done. In this case," she said more brightly, "I'm happy to report that we appear to be over the crisis. The talk I had with your father at Uncle Oliver's the other day was most instructive for both of us. He seems to have forgiven me for the worst of it and understood the rest. He should be back home soon, and then we can begin to treat each other a little more humanely in the future."

"Is that Paul's opinion, too? He's always been a great man

for having one." Alice's voice rang a bit ironically over the background chatter, but such a tone was typical of Martha's eldest.

"Oh, he's been most supportive. I couldn't have asked for better. He's driven me about, seen to my banking, kept me company, and never asked me to say more than I was prepared to tell." Then Martha admitted after a pause, "The only thing that concerns me is how all this might affect his own marriage. You know how unsound that's been of late."

"Hasn't it always?" Alice may have added a few side comments about Dorothy's character, but they were lost in the static. "If you ask me, that particular union could do with a dash of something. It's always seemed too lopsided and set in stone for my tastes."

As the eldest child, Alice had traditionally acted as the arbiter among the three siblings in their play and, later, in their lives. She liked to pronounce roundly upon her sister's superficialities, and she corresponded at length on the topic of her brother's wasted gifts. Of her own loneliness and inflexibility, she said less, though even about these she was often savagely honest. Knowing all this, Martha avoided giving her daughter too many opportunities to judge. Even her parents, at times, were fair game to Alice's ruthless devotion to the truth. In that, she often reminded Martha of Gandhi, though her mother would have never dared to tell her so.

"I only meant," Alice resumed in an effort to forestall any criticism, "that Paul has plenty of his own problems and doesn't need any help from us to make them worse. How those children of his are learning anything in the company of that woman is more than I'll ever know."

"She's not such a bad sort, all in all, and the children *are* angels."

"But as for you and Father," Alice continued less steadily, "I really shouldn't say anything at all, should I? I've always tried not to interfere too much in your lives, and now's hardly the time to start. I only wish everything could be as it once was — or, rather," she quickly corrected herself, "as it seemed to be. At least, in those days, we all believed we were happy, even though —"

"Mother!" she suddenly cried. "What are you doing? Are those pages I hear? You know how I hate it when you read while we're talking on the telephone."

"I'm sorry," Martha apologized, moving the second letter from Bombay farther away from the receiver. "It's just that I've got another note from this unhappy fellow in India, and I don't know what to do about it. And I was hoping that perhaps you might advise me."

This entreaty appealed, as the mother guessed it might, to her daughter's penchant for deciding the affairs of others as well as to her hunger for intrigue. As sober a teacher as she was, Alice was also a tireless reader of railway station kiosk mysteries and romances and sought in casual fiction some hint of the adventure that was missing from her daily life.

"What does this one have to say for itself?" she asked eagerly. "Paul told me a bit about the first and its incredible cheek, trying to threaten you with some pretend photographs and all. Has he become any more inventive by now? Do you think he's really at death's door?"

"Apparently, poor man. He was staying with his brother, Devadas, and being taken care of by him and his family, but now he's in hospital, though oddly enough he doesn't specify which one." Emboldened by her daughter's permission, Martha crackled the pages roughly between her hands and read out a synopsis of their message. "Well, there's definitely less impertinence in this, more the ramblings of a troubled man who knows he hasn't much time left. He goes over a little of what he'd written before — 'forgive me for pressing myself upon you' and 'woefully and fatally distressed' — as if he doesn't trust his English well enough to supply him with new, ready-made phrases for each occasion. No more mention of memorabilia or photographs, thank God, yet he does refer more than once to a collection of private letters."

"Yours, Mother?"

"I should say so. Listen: 'Through a large cache of letters that I was happily able to keep from the prying eyes of family,' he writes, 'I feel I've come to know you, Mrs. Houghton, almost as well as did my father. They date back over half a century, and their regularity and detail have convinced me that you and he were closer than most sisters and brothers, indeed, closer than many wives and husbands. What good fortune for the two of you to have found and kept one another, though indirectly! If only my own marriage to my poor Chanchi had fared half as well, perhaps I wouldn't be in the sorry state I am now, and I should have someone besides you and the spirit of my lost father to watch over me.'

"Pathetic, isn't it?" Martha interjected. "How alone he must feel, and how afraid!"

"So how much does he want for the lot?" Alice queried cynically.

"For the letters? Why, nothing at all! Though he does offer to send them to me," her mother paraphrased, "if I can only give him a more secure address. This is one of the reasons I rang you today, to ask if I might give him yours. Ours here is out of the question for now, what with your father's increased touchiness, and even Paul's is vulnerable, with Dorothy on hand. For her own reasons, she's sided with Samuel in this and is most likely even turning the children against me. And as for Nellie, well! But you, I thought, would understand and help me in any way you could to put this whole sad episode behind me."

During the past ten years or so, Martha and Alice hadn't seen nearly enough of each other. Work and age and distance had conspired to come between them, and their own mismatched temperaments had done the rest. From where Martha was sitting in the parlor now, she could see the last half-hearted winds of March buffeting the trees and kicking up fans of residual snow powder that glistened in the colorless air. Looking farther south over the smoking rooftops of Hedge End, she imagined the miles and miles of separating countryside, all the squares of farmland and sprouts of villages that lay between her and her first child. And she began to worry at the lengthy silence on the other end of the line.

"Dear?" she raised her voice. "That would be all right with you, wouldn't it?"

After a time, Alice said, "Well, now that you ask, I'm not altogether certain it would. To be perfectly frank, it feels off-putting to me, to act as your collaborator in this. It might have been fine with Paul — he's his own man and has his own ways — but for me it's different. I don't mean to rally around Father in any way, or oppose you, but I still shouldn't like to be the one to aid and abet an already, shall we say, ambiguous situation. Unless," she probed tentatively, "there's absolutely nothing in any of those letters that you wouldn't mind Father's seeing."

Speechless for a moment, Martha stared at her elongated reflection in the polished ebony Bakelite of the telephone and sadly shook her head. She remembered a scene from August 1914, not London gearing up for war, but the only time that she had ever met Gandhi's wife. It was at a teashop in Bayswater, and Martha and Kasturbai had hit it off fairly well, even in the presence of the man who meant so much to them both. Mrs. Gandhi was about her husband's age — forty-five — and she shared with him the slightly ailing look of those who eat too little and think too much. But, wrapped in a beautiful white sari with a floral design, she had carried herself with dignity and conversed intelligently about the weariness of travel, the coming British cold, and how much she missed her family back home. Yet, to Martha, in the clinging way in which she constantly deferred to her husband there was far too much submission on her side and far too much dominance on his. She had compared it to her own relationship with Samuel and decided that neither extreme was healthy for either women or men and that even Gandhi's great love for humanity had a few weak spots in it. The only problem was that, in a subsequent letter, she'd written half in jest, "If only you and I were married, Mohandas, you'd learn soon enough how briskly an Englishwoman treats her lover!" And it was precisely offhand comments like these that Martha thought it best to keep away from Samuel's still doubting eyes at any cost.

Returning to the present, she finally said with regret, "Not to worry, Alice, my love. I know you've only half an hour for lunch, so I won't keep you any longer. Perhaps your sister can see her way clear to helping me. All my best to your little ones."

"Mother, please, don't talk like that," Alice pleaded. "It's not that I disapprove of anything you have or haven't done. It's only a question of my trying to remain loyal to you both."

But, by then, Martha had already rung off.

One day soon after, just at the beginning of a spell of blackthorn winter, Rita Venden, the BBC *Garden Paths* expert, appeared unannounced at the Houghtons' door. She stood quaking from the cold in a smart fur toque that was hardly at home in Hedge End and a beige woolen coat that should have been longer. Her legs gleamed in silk, and Martha remembered, as she greeted her, that Rita had been one of the few in the area to sport fine stockings, even during the worst of the war's shortages.

The two women knew each other from the Darby and Joan Club, though they had seldom spoken. To Martha, there was something not quite village enough about Rita in the way she would elevate her head, even while walking alongside someone else, as if she were always peering for grander things over the horizon. Her age was a source of continuing debate as well. Easily the youngest of those neighbors who considered themselves elderly, Rita couldn't have been more than fifty-five or fifty-six, and a trim, unwrinkled specimen at that. She was currently single, but she let it be known that, like Rebecca, there had been more than one husband in her past, and more than one child, too. Yet, again like the bookseller, Rita Venden refused to be held to specifics and was instead content to be whatever her neighbors thought she was at any given moment.

At first, Martha was taken aback at the sight of her, but then she ushered the woman inside and scolded her for walking out in such a short coat on such a blustery day.

"It is a mite fresh out, isn't it, especially for this time of year?" Rita gasped as she let her wrap be taken and herself be steered nearer to the fire. "What's to become of our growing season simply doesn't bear thinking of."

"You'll have some tea?"

"With a drop of port or sherry on the side?"

Martha squinted at the clock on the mantel shelf that read half past eleven in the morning.

"Against the flu," Rita informed her in all seriousness. "The doctors in London swear it's better than any poultice."

Rebecca being at her shop, and Samuel still brooding for a

while longer up at Oliver's, the house was Martha's to do with what she would. So after brewing a pot of the bookseller's Assam and arranging a plate of lemon cakes, she poured out two glasses of the amber Jerez that was normally reserved for Sunday evenings and sat down across from her guest with an expectant look.

"Mr. Houghton is still away?" Rita began with a sharp ear lifted toward the stairwell. "It must be so lonely for you to be here without him."

"I'm comforted," Martha assured her, "by the thought that he can be at the side of his brother, who needs him so much more than I."

"That is a blessing." Miss Venden smiled at her.

"Isn't it just?"

As decorous as all this sounded, it was also partly true. By now, Martha had come to accept Samuel's absence as not so much a desertion of her as a temporary interval of caring for a brother who was in a bad way. The redefinition was mostly cosmetic, but it was the kind of instinctive give-and-take that had helped them both put up with each other through so many years.

"I always say," Rita declared, "that family is earth and water to us all. Without it, we'd be helplessly adrift and doomed to a killing solitude." She blanched slightly at her own characterization, perhaps recalling the quiet waiting for her at home. "There are limits, naturally," she amended her words with a dab at the corner of her rouged mouth. "Our loved ones are invaluable, but they must never be allowed to usurp our entire personalities. We ladies are at a particularly high risk for that and need to do all we can to maintain our integrity and our independence. Don't you agree?"

"Oh, I do," answered Martha, reminded of her own long-ago days as a suffragette.

"In my capacity as a commentator on everyday life," Rita

went on, "I'm favored with the opportunity — one might even say the duty — to notice what others take for granted, to record all the evanescent glories that everyone else passes by in a rush. Sometimes I think of myself as almost a poet, destined to be the world's spokeswoman for the truths that, without my hand, might be lost to us forever."

"I thought you broadcast only on mulches and weedicides?"

"As if that were all! Your concert of the Holst music the other night, for instance," Rita cried as if struck by the memory at random. "I mean to put it at the head of my next observations on tubers. What a pure delight that was, and how unlooked-for in such an out-of-the-way place as ours! I can't tell you how impressed I was by it all. The heavenly voices, the melodies, the hushed solemnities for a fallen hero — why, my flesh prickles at the mere thought. Feel!"

Martha declined the outstretched arm, and Rita added, "I only wish your poor Samuel could have attended along with the rest of us. I'm sure he would have appreciated the selfless nobility of the gesture as much as anyone."

The only response Martha could make was to explain how her husband's interests fell far closer to home. He was a man of local pleasures — the heft of metal in his hand, the rainy curve of a small lane toward a stand of willows — and had no need to seek any farther afield. Moreover, as involved as he had been in both war efforts, and never forgiving the sacrifice of one of his grandsons, Samuel had no truck with pacifism of any sort, not the least in the face of such monstrosities as Hitler and Mussolini. As much as he may have admired Gandhi for his ideals and been free of any jingoistic prejudices against him, Samuel had still thought him naïve, with the kind of naivety that might have endangered the whole world had it ever been let loose.

"No," she concluded, coming back to the discussion at

hand, "I'm afraid my husband wouldn't have taken too well to the other night's proceedings. He's never been one for fussing over any individual, whatever his station. He thinks it steals too much thunder away from all the rest."

"Whereas you," Rita Venden probed gently over the last of her sherry, "have always prided yourself on a more penetrating view, haven't you? I know that you and Rebecca Pye, for example, have acted for some time now as our unofficial avant-garde in the way of new and exotic ideas. In fact, if it weren't for your enlightened efforts, I can't imagine how dismal our prospects would be here in Hedge End. Mind you, I've nothing but the greatest respect for village life," she claimed. "It's quiet and healthy and filled with good fellowship. But the intellect needs more, doesn't it, certainly in these modern times? And we all feel that you, along with a very few others, have been instrumental in providing us with a window onto the larger world that we so sorely need."

"How kind of you! But let's not overlook your own contributions," Martha said as graciously as she could. "Your studies of perennials and proper hoeing techniques —"

"Yes, yes, one does what one can." Rita nodded after a modest interlude. Then she shifted in her chair and said more pointedly, "But what good fortune it must have been for you actually to have known the great man himself for so long and through so many changing circumstances. What was it, then? Almost sixty years of visits and correspondence, confidences and the like? At least, that's what's being said around town."

Martha stared at her. "By whom, might I ask?"

"Oh, it's all in the breeze, scattered abroad like so many seedlings through the air. Now who was it mentioned it to me first?" Rita feigned to ask herself. "Was it the good doctor? No, he'd never. Mr. Cobb, perhaps? Or might it have been Rebecca Pye or even your own Samuel, that time I ran into him coming out of her bookshop? But no matter!" Rita sat aggressively forward, setting aside her former restraint. "What I and my fellow writers want to know, Martha, are the facts, the naked and unashamed facts. The who, what, where, when, and how of your secret relationship with Gandhi. The public just now is seething to know, and it's my obligation to inform them to the best of my abilities. As I was saying to my associates in the church during your performance, there's news even in the most backward locations, as long as one is willing to ferret it out. In your case, I think we'd best start with a fairly straightforward review of the start of the affair. How old were you at the time?" She ticked off questions on her long, insect fingers. "How old was he, what level of intimacy did you reach and when, how many other men had you known before?"

"I really don't think I'd care to —" Martha objected feebly.

"Oh, don't be shy. All of history's most celebrated men have had their inamoratas and their liaisons. Why should the Indian have been any different?" From nowhere she suddenly produced a leather notebook and a pencil, not unlike Constable Pratt's, and at once began jotting down symbols and abbreviations. "Now, if you don't mind my asking, how was it you were able to keep your amour hidden from your lawful husband over so many years? Was it because Mr. Houghton didn't care enough to notice, or was it only the result of the substantial distances involved?" Rita lifted the pencil to her cheek and grew more reflective. "Or perhaps what our listeners and readers would be most captivated by is the issue of race. Would Samuel," she asked in a clinical tone, "have been less troubled by it all if the other man had been white? Or was it the dark skin that attracted you to Gandhi in the first place?"

As she prattled madly on, Martha experienced a sense of

physical plummeting as if the cushion beneath her were sagging through the floor. Her face grew hot, and her breath came short, and a curious distortion of her vision seemed to bring a huge, invisible thumb into the confines of the room.

"Rita, please," she finally begged with her hands raised in defense. "I can't tell you anything, not now or ever. It's simply too, too private. If you have any decency, you'll agree that some things are best left unsaid."

At this, the journalist sat stunned, seemingly unable to believe that anyone should balk at such a reasonable request for information. "But didn't Gandhi himself give his life for the truth?" she demanded. "And wouldn't it be a gross betrayal of his memory for you to confess anything less?"

Martha rose slowly from her chair until she attained a greater height and glared down at her guest.

"I'll thank you to leave my house this instant, Miss Venden, and never darken its doorway again." She stood back a pace to allow the younger woman to pass, but then she effectively herded her out of the house. "And I'll caution you," Martha finished, perhaps more ominously than she intended, "not to encourage such slander of a good woman's name, unless you want an immediate action brought against you. Now, good day!"

At the door, Rita turned to take a parting shot and almost struck noses with Martha.

"I fear you're woefully mistaken, Mrs. Houghton, if you think you've heard the last of this," she stammered as she tried to button her coat against the winds. "We in the fourth estate aren't so readily shaken off, once we've sunk our teeth into something ripe."

And in that, if in nothing else, she was right.

8

FOR MARTHA, and to a lesser degree for Samuel and the rest of the Houghton family, the month of April 1948 was unsettled and hard. The climate itself seemed to be of two minds. One day the skies would appear as churned as dishwater, the clouds like yeasty batter and the air smelling of wet metal. Then the people of Hedge End would grumble their way from errand to errand with their shoulders bent inward and their arms clapped to their sides like penguins. Yet the next day would dawn cold but dazzling, and then everyone would remember that seasons always change, sooner or later, and they would put off going home just to contemplate a shining pool in a ditch. On days like these, when rumors spread of robins, Martha would venture outdoors for an hour or two, if only to visit the Olympia or to pick up some fabric ordered from London. But before long she would be startled by a glint of light that might have been a flashbulb in a passing car window or from the depths of some stinging nettles, and she would scurry back to the house with her kerchief or coat covering one side of her face. Her curtains remained closed on the sunniest days, as her fears of being hounded by the press made her an invalid in her own life.

Samuel's return in the second week of the month might have helped ease the pressure, but what was left of his moodiness kept him mostly alone in the toolshed. Martha was dumbfounded on the morning when he walked through the front door and, without a word to her, headed straight out the back and since then had rarely been seen, except at meals and bedtime. At Oliver's, Samuel had seemed so compassionate and accepting that she'd assumed all was over. Gandhi was gone forever, each of Martha's past sins had been brought out into the open, their worst marital storm had been weathered, and now everything should have been returning to the placid state of a couple in the twilight of their lives. Yet Samuel still talked to her as sparingly as possible and forever found excuses to be in some other part of the house every time she needed him. It felt as if he had forgiven her and he had not, as if he were straining unnaturally after some false resolution, when all the while fragments of insecurity and bitterness were still lying scattered around him, waiting to be glued back together again. Or his stay at Oliver's was the trial and the sentencing, but his homecoming was the punishment.

On her side, Martha, too, was becoming inevitably accustomed to their new situation. She accepted her virtual widowhood, first because she was sure it wouldn't last, and then because it gave her more time to take stock. In those moments when she was completely honest with herself, she had to concede that her old friend's death had not yet reached her as it should have. Rather, its impact seemed to have been delayed, as though it were still in transit from India, stalled somewhere en route. She missed Gandhi and his faithful letters, she commiserated with his son's condition, and she regretted her own prolonged duplicity. But the stark reality of his murder and her loss had still to be brought home to her. And now, with all the world being invited to share in her private grief, she began to worry if it ever would.

For Rita Venden's final words had been no idle threat. Representatives of various newspapers did, indeed, descend upon the village in the hopes of persuading Martha to tell her story. The residents, some of whom put them up in their houses at outrageous prices, had little trouble identifying them. The journalists announced their presence either by their look — city-dressed, restless, driving powerful cars, and bored with the simpler things — or by their insincerity. They never asked anyone a question about business or pastimes without a second, stealthier question lurking in the background. And whenever the greengrocer wanted to know what brand of chocolate they preferred or the proprietress of the Eglantine let them sample a new tea, their eyes would focus past one's ear as they searched for some figure who was more obviously newsworthy. There was an infinite cruelty in their professional detachment and in the dissatisfaction they always felt with any too mundane truth. "Are you absolutely certain of that?" was their favorite refrain, as if absolute certainty were as easy to come by as sharpened pencils. Yet, even when they were cited chapter and verse or were shown recent photographs of Martha attending baptisms and garden parties, they continued to seek out corroborating witnesses at the next door and then the next. A pervading spirit of falseness seemed to have trailed them into Hedge End, until the villagers themselves started looking at one another with hooded, skeptical eyes.

If the reporters had arrived all at once, in a horde as it

were, the onslaught might have been more bearable. Martha might have been done with them in a single interview or conference and thought no more about it. But they came in dribs and drabs, one week a rude young man from the nearby *Southern Daily Echo* and the following a girl with glasses from the *Portsmouth News,* then a Brighton couple from the *Evening Argus* and a silver-haired gentleman out of the *Daily Herald.* They eventually positioned themselves around the Houghton property like so many surveyors' rods — one itching among the rosebushes, another glum behind the dustbin, a third and a fourth exchanging signals across the thawing yard. At first, Martha had found their nearness offensive, even frightening. She'd tried to shoo them away with a broom, then called upon Constable Pratt to escort the trespassers out of her sight. But, as time passed and the journalists rotated in shifts, she came to accept their presence, though never to the point of granting any of them an exclusive. She understood, however, that they were only doing their work, and she finally learned their first names and greeted them from her window. A rather shy fellow from Plymouth's *Western Morning News* one mild afternoon actually helped her air a rug on a line and confided in her his concerns about his fiancée, who was having second thoughts.

Away from the house, unfortunately, was a different story. At those times when Martha had to walk to the shops for food or thread or merely wanted to be out and about, a gauntlet of inquiries and suggestive asides, and not all of them from outsiders, inevitably awaited her.

"Allow me to tell you, my dear," the postmistress would whisper to her with a smirk, "how sorry I feel for your situation. It must be so difficult to have come so close to world renown, only to have lost it in the end."

Or Mrs. Boon, the seamstress who disliked Martha anyway for making most of her own clothes, would nod to her at the door of the flower shop, ask her out of the blue any number of technical questions about Indian marriage customs, and then look offended when she didn't know the answers.

And once even Price Hindes accompanied his wrapping of tinned meats with the observation, "Vegetarians, they say, haven't enough animal fire in them to support normal, ahem, relations. Is that so?"

In the end, the infection spread throughout the village until it circled back into her own home. One forenoon Samuel, in passing morosely from the kitchen to the bedroom upstairs, wondered aloud if Martha hadn't yet tired of all the attention.

"Of course, I have," she answered him shortly from her chair. "But what am I to do about it, I'd like to know?"

Her husband shrugged at the foot of the steps while staring down at the floor between them. "If you were to ask me, and I realize you don't care to, I'd say you should choose one of the herd and tell him what he wants to hear. Give him the whole scoop," he said, "as the Americans like to call it. Then you — then we — might at least be left in peace."

"I can't see why I should give them the pleasure —" Martha began.

"Because if you don't, they'll take it anyway!"

"— over something that's none of their business. Besides," she went on, shrinking back with a bob of her head, "I shouldn't know where to begin. Or end. How does one encapsulate a half-century friendship that never had any of the characteristics of an ordinary acquaintance? I'd always be afraid that I wasn't doing it justice, that I'd be betraying a good man who never deserved all the hatred and violence that were turned against him. I don't think I could live with myself, if anything I said might be misconstrued or twisted out of shape. I feel I owe him something better than that. I feel we all do, in a way.

"I know, Samuel," Martha concluded, lowering her voice, "that this must be so difficult for you to endure or even begin to understand. I know I've treated you shabbily, and I shouldn't blame you if you never spoke to me again. But that would be wrong, both for us after so many years together and for his memory. No," she decided at last, "I think in this case that silence is best and that I shouldn't tell any of the reporters a blessed word. Then they'll have nothing whatsoever to write."

Something in her quiet, measured words finally seemed to move him, and for the first time in weeks Samuel showed her the ghost of a smile.

"True," he agreed in one long syllable as he wearily mounted the stairs. "But have you ever considered what they might do to his legacy — not to mention your reputation — if you sit back and let them imagine the worst?"

Then he dragged himself up to bed, from where, in a few minutes, his wife could hear him begin to wheeze.

Rita Venden couldn't believe her good luck, not only in having been invited back to the Houghtons' front parlor, but also in being asked to bring her new tape recorder along with her. To Martha, it seemed, even the rudest Hedge Ender was better than a stranger.

"You see," she said breathlessly as she waved the honeycomb head of the microphone before Martha's face, "it's like I was telling Jonathan, my producer, only last week. People are people, and they all want the same thing, their moment in the sun. Give them a soapbox and an audience, and they'll take to the opportunity like a bird to the air. And all this is accomplished through the magic of magnetic tape" — here she laid a trembling hand on her recorder — "and the voices it captures inside its little box. Isn't it a marvel, though?"

In fact, the apparatus was cumbersome and hard to operate, and when it did function it gave off a smell of smoking rubber. But Rita maintained that it was the latest model available — the G.E.C. or some such abbreviation — and assured her subject that none of the reptilian hisses and pops coming out of the speaker would interfere with the sound reproduction. She had only to pass the microphone back and forth between them without awakening too much static, though this caution soon had both their heads oscillating on either side of it like the escapement pallet in a clock.

"Now, Martha," Rita said sweetly, "there's absolutely no reason for you to be nervous. I'll just switch this on — so! — and we'll begin with a few simple establishing questions." She consulted the opened notebook on her lap. "So when and where exactly did you and Mr. Gandhi meet? How did it happen, and how did it make you feel? Tell me everything you can remember."

During the course of the next hour or so, Martha patiently reviewed her life, not perhaps in perfect detail, but as plainly and forthrightly as she could. She told of her long association with Gandhi, of their letters and telephone calls, of their meetings during his five journeys to England, of all the thoughts they had shared. Much to her surprise, the experience of unburdening herself of so many recollections was easier and more liberating than she'd ever expected it to be. Martha rather took to the act of self-revelation and before long found a host of treasures in her past that she hadn't even suspected. That time in November 1906 was one, when she and Gandhi had dined privately in a side room of the

Criterion Restaurant in Piccadilly Circus. This meeting had been during his briefest visit to England, when the thirty-seven-year-old lawyer had come up from South Africa to plead for greater justice for his fellow Indians in the Transvaal. At that stage in his career, he had yet to adopt his later guise of poverty and still appeared in the streets of London as the suited European he thought would make a stronger case before the House of Commons. Yet, over the vegetarian meal that he was so eager for his friend to try, his dark mustache had twitched mischievously, and his quick fingers had plucked at his companion's bean salad with all the playfulness of a boy.

"Yet were you never privy," Rita interrupted her train of thought, "to any state secrets or communiqués about his plans to bring the Empire to its knees and break its hold on India? Only think," she urged the other woman, "how privileged your position was! To have been so close for so long to someone who actually changed the world, changed the entire world! How many of our listeners could say the same?"

"But it was nothing like that," Martha objected. "The friendship we had was always more personal, more everyday." Troubled by Rita's unbridled enthusiasm, she sat forward to make her point more clearly. "As involved as he was in all his separate causes," she continued, "our conversations and letters always seemed somehow smaller, less worldly. I'm not saying that we didn't discuss the issues of the day as they came and went over the span of fifty-some years. We did, and quite exhaustively. It would have been strange if we hadn't. But, at the time, we thought we had more important matters to talk about — our spouses and our children, our health, how beastly cold it was where I lived and how beastly hot it was where he lived, and yet how equally wet in both places. These are what concerned us more than anything else, not the headlines that the papers and the newsreels kept harping on, but the same daily affairs that busy everybody. That's probably what made our friendship so long-lasting, the fact that it was no more exceptional than anyone else's. I'm sorry," Martha said, reaching out in genuine sympathy, "that I don't have any very provocative disclosures for you, but I certainly can't recall what never happened. That wouldn't be fair to him or me or your audience. I do hope this doesn't present too much of a problem."

"Well," Rita whimpered, visibly hungering for more, "I suppose if you can't, you can't."

She looked so let down that Martha added helpfully, "Four or five years ago we did exchange a series of letters when his wife lay dying in a Bombay prison."

"In a prison, you say?"

"For doing something or other to gain independence," Martha told her. "Oddly enough, though, the political struggle didn't seem the worst to him. By then, he'd grown so used to it that it had almost become an annual ritual. But the poor man was so torn with indecision over whether to allow his wife to eat meat or take penicillin that he finally even turned to me for advice."

"And what did you tell him?" the reporter prompted her.

"What could I say?" Martha protested. "Being British, Western, to me it's always seemed foolish not to hold onto life at whatever cost. I think I wrote him that he must make up his own mind in such a private concern — and, naturally, let her make up hers, as well as she could in her delirium — but that I myself would never wish to give up while there was still a breath left in my body. If he had any fault, perhaps it was there," she reflected with an unseeing stare at the recorder grinding hoarsely between them. "He sometimes loved souls more than the people who owned them. He thought that our lives should be well lost for truth, whereas the rest of us would probably rather lose them for more personal things — our families, our friends, love."

"Ah!" Rita Venden almost sprang out of her chair, every one of her investigative senses on the alert. "Now this sounds a bit more promising. There's nothing that can reach my listeners' hearts faster, you know, than romance. Do tell me more."

"I'm afraid being romantic" — Martha paused to search for the right words — "was really the furthest thing from our minds. We always treated each other more like sister and brother than lovers, the way we used to share the sort of confidences that we wouldn't share with anyone else. I think he knew Samuel and I knew his wife — he called her 'Ba' — almost better than we knew them ourselves. I only wish," Martha lamented, "that he'd tried to do a little more to save her."

"Are you saying," Rita pressed her, "that this poor lady actually went to her grave without ever knowing of your close relationship with her husband? Is that how you now wish it could have been for Mr. Houghton, too, if you hadn't decided to go public? And what about the children, the most innocent victims in any such case?" she went on, her honeyed concern sounding flat and hollow. "Do you think any of them has been injured by your actions? He still has a number of sons living over there, doesn't he?"

For another twenty minutes, Martha dodged and backtracked before the terrier interviewer, always on guard against misspeaking or betraying Gandhi's memory. Nothing of any great moment was divulged, though the correspondent seemed pleased with what she heard and even fretted over whether or not she would have enough tape. In the end, the two women parted almost as friends, Rita feeling proud of having bested her male colleagues and Martha feeling free of guilt at last.

Next Sunday, just as Samuel was preparing to retreat to his shed, Martha invited him to stay in with her and listen to the special edition of *Garden Paths*. The interview, she vowed, would answer most of his lingering doubts, and then they could both get back to being the way they were before.

"I must say I think I acquitted myself rather well," she boasted as she made toast and cocoa, as excitedly as if they were courting again. "You were right, as usual. It was much better to have done with it, once and for all. And it really was far less distressing than I'd imagined. Miss Venden can be perfectly charming when she puts her mind to it. Or," Martha corrected herself, adopting Samuel's typical cynicism to please him, "when she has something to gain."

When the program finally began and *"Mrs. Houghton"* was introduced, Martha herself suddenly cried out, "My Lord, Samuel! Don't tell me that's what my voice sounds like to others."

"To perfection." He nodded, chuckling in spite of his uneasiness.

"Then I'll never again blame you for not wanting to talk to me. I'll insist upon it!" And this exaggerated reference to their recent quarrel helped both husband and wife put most of the last few weeks behind them.

The interview progressed as uneventfully as it had at its recording, and Martha was gratified to see her husband's calm reaction. Samuel sipped at his cup more slowly and steadily than usual, to warm his throat or perhaps to hide the telltale flickers around his mouth. He wouldn't want his wife to think that he approved of what she had done or of the spectacle she was making of herself, first in Hedge End and now throughout the entire country. A man as quick to feel offenses as he was had a certain shellacked reserve to keep intact. Still, for all his scowls and simulated interest in the crease of his trousers, Martha could tell that he was secretly thrilled to hear someone who was so much a part of him being broadcast as if she were a movie star or a politician.

It was not until the last third of the program that a change came over the two voices contained inside the wireless. Gaps began to appear between questions and answers, and surface cracks and rustlings took the place of clear syllables. Whereas before Martha had marveled at the unfamiliar tenor of her voice, now she found it hard to understand how the words she heard herself speaking could possibly have been hers.

Yet there was Rita Venden, saying as clearly as though she now sat between them, *"After a short break to mark the hour, please return to hear more of Martha Houghton's"* — and here came the other voice to finish the sentence with the teasing phrase — *"very provocative disclosures!"*

Then, just as Martha was wondering if it was the cocoa or the interview that was making her cheeks burn so red, she heard her next response to a query about her friendship with Gandhi. *"We didn't discuss the issues of the day as they came and went over the span of fifty-some years,"* the tape insisted. *"We thought we had more important matters to talk about."*

"Such as?" asked the journalist right on cue.

"Our conversations and letters are what concerned us more than anything else," Martha's voice replied, though in a somewhat disembodied style. *"That's probably what made our friendship so long-lasting, the fact that it was more exceptional than anyone else's."*

Martha looked frantically from the wireless to her husband and back.

"Is there something wrong?" Samuel worried.

"But I didn't —"

"Shh! We're missing it."

They both bent closer.

"*. . . sure all my listeners are asking themselves now,*" Rita Venden seemed to hiccup out in a storm of static, "*is how far did matters progress between you, Martha, and the Indian martyr before his untimely demise. Even given the distances involved, not to mention the separate lives and families you were both caught up in, it must have been inevitable that at some point deeper feelings than just mere friendship should have developed between you.*"

"*Well, Miss Venden —*"

"I never called her that!"

"*Being romantic, we did exchange a series of letters when his wife lay dying in a Bombay prison.*"

"*Truly?*" Rita sounded suitably, if melodramatically, shocked. "*Do you think that was proper, given your respective situations? Wouldn't it have been wiser to have acted toward each other only as sister and brother?*"

"*Oh, no,*" the electronic Martha declared in a confession that instantly filled the parlor, "*we always treated each other more like lovers.*"

Mercifully, the charade went on for only a few more minutes, during which time Martha literally could not bring herself to raise her head. The room around her had long since lost its anchor and bucked about like a picnic blanket in a gale, dizzying her until her vision blurred. Even without seeing her husband's face, she could feel his anger, the injured lowering of the eyes that would make it impossible for him to look directly at her. Their long lifetime together seemed to concentrate in a rush of noise in her ears, and she despaired of ever being believed again, much less loved. Yet, when she finally glanced at him, she saw that Samuel was only wearing the sour grimace that he usually reserved for gamblers and music hall singers.

"The woman's a charlatan!" he scoffed. "A mountebank, a damned manipulator of switches and dials. I shouldn't be at all surprised if the BBC hands her her walking papers before the end of the week. No reputable firm is going to stand for such shenanigans, not for very long. Why, they'd find themselves served with slander suits every hour on the hour!"

"You don't believe, then," Martha peered up at him gratefully, "that I said any of those awful words, at least not in that way?"

Samuel crossed the rug between them and bent over his wife as far as his arthritis would let him.

"Martha," he began, "I've known you for over fifty years, for nearly three-quarters of your life. Don't you think I'd recognize your real sentiments when I heard them?"

He reached to one side to turn off the wireless in the middle of its biographical sketch of Miss Rita Venden. As always, the set took a few seconds to cool down, popping and clicking with a not unpleasant whiff of ozone.

"Now, why don't you come upstairs with me to rest?" he said as gallantly as he had ever said anything. "I've missed that in our Sunday afternoons, haven't you?"

For the remainder of that day and into the evening, the Houghtons were observed by various outside sources, sitting or passing together as shadows in their upstairs window. Speculation ran wildly through Hedge End about their future, and some of the news services even went so far as to contact the couple's children by telephone. Such an early darkening of the bedroom light, the reporters suggested, might mean anything.

9

ON THE FOLLOWING TUESDAY, Samuel surprised Martha once again by appearing in the kitchen with a pair of suitcases from the shed out back.

"Do you think these will be enough?" he asked her.

"Enough for what?"

"For our holiday."

"We're both retired, Samuel," Martha reminded him. "We're always on holiday."

In answer, her husband pulled back the curtain and made a face toward the privet hedge at the end of the lawn.

"I just found a man with a notebook in his hand," he said with a sigh, "squatting in the manure we use for fertilizer. Don't you think it's time we left town before one of them gets seriously hurt?"

Now it was Martha's turn to be skeptical. By this late date, she knew something of the ways in which long marriages healed and didn't heal. Injuries and grudges and even outright ruptures between lifetime companions recovered at a rate that was different from those of younger couples. Whereas a pair of newlyweds might salve a wound with a night out on the town and by staying up until dawn, the Houghtons had their own set of remedies. They made cups of tea for each other, they massaged shoulders and feet, they talked about neutral subjects in the past, and they reached out for each other in the dark, pretending to be only stretching overworked muscles. The convalescence rarely progressed smoothly, but flared and ebbed in fits and starts, moving from forgiveness to further condemnation as easily as it had just finished moving from accusation to forgiveness. Glances, pursed lips, the random appearance of meaningful names or even initials — anything could spark a setback and a return to a previous fever. Today, Martha was prepared to let Samuel take the lead, for the time being, but she reserved her doubts about his sincerity and his hidden motives. There were still too many tics and grumbles in him.

"If you say so, dear," she agreed at last, beginning to clear the breakfast table. "And I'll even let you surprise me with our destination. Are you happy now?"

In a burst of activity the likes of which they hadn't known in years, Martha and Samuel packed, rang for tickets, stole away under cover of darkness, and were on their way to Portsmouth before their neighbors even missed them. It was Samuel's plan to keep them on the move for a week or so, just long enough for the press to lose interest and find someone else to harass. "You'll be yesterday's news before we even reach London," he told his wife on the night train as they watched the sleeping countryside fly past them. "And, by the time we're home again, even Rita Venden will have grown tired of asking you questions about your Gandhi.

"Did you know, by the way, that the poor fellow spent some two thousand three hundred and thirty-eight days in Indian and South African prisons? Imagine that!" cried Samuel in what sounded like honest admiration. "Almost six and a half years in total out of a man's life, and all for his ideals. I wonder how many of us could do the same for any cause or reason whatsoever?"

"Where in the world did you learn such a thing?" Martha asked him warily.

"Oh, just from some little reading I've been doing lately. A book here, a book there."

They would need to avoid, Samuel reasoned, their own children's homes, for they were probably already being staked out by local stringers and freelance photographers. But that didn't mean they should miss certain nostalgic places altogether, as long as they visited them circumspectly and in private.

"All these recent events," he mused over their thermos of tea, "have most likely started you reminiscing, as they have me. I never had a chance to know your aunt Feemy, but she sounds like a brave soul, about as good as any you could have found in those days. And, well, it's occurred to me that, by getting to know more about where you've come from, I just might prove to be a better husband for you than I've been lately."

"That's sweet of you," said Martha with a trace of suspicion. "But it's not really necessary, is it?"

Her husband shrugged and gazed out the window.

"Shouldn't we be doing something to renew ourselves," he murmured thoughtfully, "now that spring's almost here?"

Portsmouth seemed to have readied itself for their visit. After a station breakfast and a nap at their boarding house, the two struck out for a day of sightseeing around Martha's old neighborhood. Inescapably, much had changed since her youth, and she found the experience more than a little sobering. Age had affected everything, decaying wood and stone alike, while the war still festered in closed alleys and in the adult stares of the children. Yet, for all that, the tang of sea air and the play of light, almost bottle green in its freshness, were identical to what they'd always been. The doors, too, wore the same warped expressions as before, the roofs lay saturated by chronic fogs, and even the most landlocked roads rang with unseen bells from long ago. In time, Martha became a girl again, hurrying along with her husband from one corner to the next and supplying a museum docent's monologue about every cul-de-sac and vestibule they came across. The day, happily, was ideal for such activities. The white sun and the salty wind bustled them from street to street with the same carelessness that it used on tatters of paper, blown coiling in midair.

Aunt Feemy's house, as Martha had known for some time, had been taken over by a marine insurance firm, and the chintz curtains had been replaced by blinds and desk lamps with shades of emerald and gold. Samuel urged his wife to lift the brass knocker and ask the men inside if she might see her old room again, but she said she'd rather not. It was enough, she told him, for her to pass by the open windows and remember. Her husband was only too glad to follow her about, partaking of her excitement and a youthfulness that he hadn't seen in her for years. As much as Martha sometimes distrusted the excesses that nostalgia was prone to, she still treasured all the memories, both good and bad, that had gone into making up the life that seemed to be receding further away from her every day.

Finally, toward the latter part of the afternoon, she came upon a living relic that she could hardly believe still existed. Hanging out from beneath a set of ecru blinds, an impossibly old woman sat with her milky, blind eyes trained on the clamor of boats and waves at the bottom of the lane. When Martha saw her, she stopped in her tracks, then inched closer as if she were afraid of disturbing a mirage.

"Mother Mead, isn't it? Mother Gertie Mead?"

"Who's there? Penelope? Have you brought me my ciggies?"

Martha reached up to grasp her hand. "No, it's Martha, Martha Weekes," she said in an unconsciously childish singsong. "The same girl who used to read to you at her aunt's of a summer's evening. Don't you remember?

"Even then," she whispered to her husband out of the corner of her mouth, "her eyes weren't all that good, from the sail-mending she used to do, though I thought at the time she was only trying to hide the fact that she couldn't read."

"Martha?" cried the woman in the window. "Oh, no, no, you can't be any Martha that I ever knew. The only one I can think of must be gone a long, long time now."

"But I was less than half your age at the time! You were forty years old, or even older, almost sixty years ago," Martha calculated, "and I was only a child. If anyone should be surprised at our meeting again, it should be I."

This much was true. Mrs. Mead claimed to be ninety-six or ninety-seven — the latter on her bad days — and had survived more wars and spouses and offspring than anyone could count. Time had taken her sight from her, as well as her legs, and left her as worn as a bollard on the quay. Yet she still argued that the passerby simply couldn't be that studious girl who used to live in the red brick boarding house.

"She disappeared with a foreigner, as I understood it," Gertie Mead nodded wisely down at them. "Took herself off overseas with him, never to be heard from in these parts again. Went to China or India or one of those faraway places. I recall that I began to miss her as soon as she was gone."

With a hand on her husband's chest, to steady herself or to calm him, Martha tried to explain to the old woman how her memory must be playing tricks on her. She was confusing one incident with another and elaborating it beyond all proportion. But Mother Mead still refused to be put off her particular version of the past.

"What a lovely couple they made," she burbled on with her face turned into the wind, "strolling the quays and sharing a tea and holding hands in the twilight. It's a shame they never came back to see us again."

Such an awkward beginning to their vacation was hardly what Martha thought her husband had had in mind. Yet Samuel only smiled indulgently at the blind woman's toothless maunderings and proceeded with the best will in the world on a trek that should have made him feel ill at ease. He seemed to be enjoying their review of his wife's distant youth even more than she.

"You know," he said as they settled in for the night beneath a patchwork eiderdown, "I think we should go the whole hog and take in Ventnor as well. What do you say? Shall we ship across to the island tomorrow and pick up a few mementos for the grandchildren?"

For all her misgivings, Martha meekly assented and kissed Samuel good night. She would rather have attempted a surreptitious visit to Nellie in Southsea, but an early morning telephone call to her daughter dissuaded her from that. As during her latest talk with Alice, the voice on the other end of the line reached her as small and muted, even though its being so much closer should have made it sound less faint.

"You're here?" Nellie responded somewhat skeptically. "Both you and Father? Together? Does anyone else know?"

"We're near." Martha felt the need to withhold the specifics. "And we were just asking ourselves if we shouldn't pop on down for a day to see you and Peter. And Frederick, too," she said at once, then lied, "We have gifts for everyone!"

Nellie told Martha that her son-in-law wasn't there, as he was rarely at home, traveling incessantly as he did to sell and distribute something or other to do with industrial chemicals. Nellie's was one of those marriages that worked best when it worked least. She had no interest whatsoever in her husband's trade, as he had no comprehension of how anyone who stayed at home all day could possibly call herself busy. Yet, in truth, his wife never rested. At the age of forty-five, coiffed, candied, and perfectly coordinated, with a daughter at Harrods and a sixteen-year-old son still chafing at home, Nellie was forever straightening coverlets that were already true, gardening, painting fences, and keeping appointments at hairdressers' and tearooms with a sacred regularity. No one, her husband included, had ever caught her lying down in the middle of the day, and not even her mother knew the full extent of her civic duties and associations. Absolutely everyone admired her.

Yet today she seemed strangely defensive, until Martha asked her, "Have you been at all badgered about me and my situation, dear? Any newspapers or BBC people? I hope you didn't put any stock in that silly Sunday interview, if you even heard it."

"We've had some bother. A few calls, one or two knocks on the door during dinner, and yesterday I think a man took Peter's picture when I picked him up from school." Nellie hesitated, and her mother thought she could hear the fiery rasp of cellophane being wrapped about leftovers. "It's nothing we can't handle," she went on, "but we'd really rather wish we didn't have to. What have you got yourself into now, Martha? Anything that might have lasting repercussions for the rest of us?"

"I don't think so," Martha replied, momentarily nonplussed as she always was whenever Nellie called her by her name. The echo of that "now" reminded Martha that this daughter, too, had something of her father's judgmental nature. "But, whatever the case may be," she continued, "your father and I don't suppose this can go on much longer. Once the press finds that they can't get hold of me at their leisure, they're bound to turn to other, weaker prey. Then we can all breathe more easily and put all this behind us."

"But can we ever, do you think?"

"What, dear?"

"Put all this behind us? Completely, I mean."

"Now you're beginning to sound like Alice," Martha noted after falling silent for a time.

"Would that be so wrong?" wondered Nellie. Again certain kitchen sounds intruded, drawers of jostling knives and the gulp of pipes beneath the sink. Then she said, "It's not the end of the world, I know, and I shouldn't want to overstate anything or follow the crowd in its thinking. But revelations *are* revelations, whether they take place in private or in public, and once they're exposed they can never be covered up again. I'm only asking if you thought all this through sufficiently, Mother, before you called in the reporters."

Martha thought she knew where her daughter was heading and considered just ringing off, glad that she and Samuel hadn't gone down to Southsea, when Nellie concluded, "And, besides, I can't conceive what you were hoping to get out of the association from the start. It's not as if the rest of us haven't dreamt of daring something along the same lines," her daughter breathed in a lower register, "or even gone so far as to plan it, only to see our courage fail us at the last moment. So few of our lives, sadly, turn out as we'd have liked."

Once Martha had said goodbye and started for the stairs to help Samuel pack again, the residue of her daughter's final words began to nag at her. Was it really jealousy that she had detected in her voice? Could it be that Nellie was longing for the life of a woman nearly twice her age who had distinguished herself more for her repeated mistakes than for anything else? How miserably I must have failed her, grieved Martha as she entered the room, to have left her no one better to envy in the world than me! And, for the first time, the true meaning of Gandhi's horror of rebirth came over her as she felt how dreadful it would be to have to live all of this again.

The Houghtons caught the afternoon packet to the island and were grateful for the off-season abundance of inside places. For the wind was rising, and tall, black clouds were coming on.

On this, their fourth excursion to the Isle of Wight, slumped against the boat's coamings and staring dully out at the slate-colored waves scalloping past, Samuel seemed to be engulfed by his overcoat and anchored to the bench by the weight of its black wool. Watching over him, Martha was saddened to see how much smaller and thinner he'd grown even in the past few days. Or, perhaps, she was only now noticing how terribly ancient they had both become. Her husband's face, in the cold sea light, looked fibrous and pasty, the cheeks deflated and the damp eyes ringed with dark circles. He might have been made of paper, for all the hard substance that was left in him. Yet Martha could remember, as if it had been as recent as this morning, a time when his hair had been blue-black and full, his back as straight as a rod, and his gait a long stride, before his joints had swollen and stuck. Sometimes she forgot that the boy of twenty-four was still contained somewhere within the grandfather of seventy-five, lost in the complex depths of his life as inextricably as he now was in the folds of his coat.

Suddenly, Martha noticed the corner of a book peeking out from one of his pockets. For Samuel to read anything at all other than his bulky motor journals was unusual enough. But for him to have brought something with them on their holiday was simply unprecedented.

"What are you reading?" she asked him over the slap and rasp of the packet over the sea.

"What? Oh, nothing, really." He sheepishly tucked the book farther down into his coat and thereby automatically doubled his wife's curiosity. "Only a little book that I just happened to pick up the other day."

Martha poked at him and poked at him until she was finally able to free the volume from his pocket. Then she stared wide-eyed down at the title.

"*The Song Celestial*?" she cried out. "But isn't this a translation of the *Bhagavad Gita*?"

"Well, I don't know how it's pronounced exactly, yet I suppose you'd know more about that than I would."

"But what on earth are you doing with it, Samuel? You can't be reading it!"

At this, her husband sat up straighter, took back his book, and assumed an offended air. "And why not, I'd like to know? Do you think that you and Rebecca Pye and Gandhi and all that crowd are the only ones who have any interest in such things? I did go to school, Martha," Samuel chided her, half in anger and half in chagrin, "a few years of it, at any rate. And I have always had some inclination toward thinking of such things. Not in any organized way, you understand, as in a church or even in a prayer meeting, but in here." And he pointed to his sunken chest beneath the overcoat. "Especially as I come closer and closer to my own end. I expect I'd only like to know a bit more about what's waiting for me there, if anything is."

"But are you making head or tail of it at all?" Martha asked him. "As I recall, it's not that easy going, even for an expert."

Pausing to ride out the swell of the currents as the boat nosed toward the rising and falling Spithead off Ryde, Samuel said he thought that he was.

"As I see it, it's first of all a poem about a man's or a woman's work and duty and what it takes to perform them on the battleground of life. I'm not too far off, am I?" he asked in a breath that stuttered with self-consciousness. "There's a lot more to it, no doubt, but I haven't finished reading and studying every page yet. Then there's that whole matter of souls and birth and death and rebirth. I can't follow that very well, but it intrigues me. The possibility that perhaps we in the West might be looking at it all wrong, as through the wrong end of a telescope, seeing everything so much smaller and more individual than it really is. What if life and death," Samuel said weakly with his eyes trained on the restless ocean, "aren't as separate and opposite as they appear to be, but are only like the crest and the trough of one wave or the two sides of the same coin? So what's the coin, then? Well, perhaps if we all understood that better, we wouldn't always end up being so selfish and afraid of everything and everybody. Am I getting closer to it, do you think?"

Before Martha could ask him what he was trying to accomplish with this new tack of his, her husband said, "Did you know that Gandhi's wife died on the twenty-second of the month and that on the twenty-second of every month after that he had the entire text of this poem recited out loud in her honor? I wonder, Martha, if you and I haven't underestimated the man in some ways, both in his public and his private lives. Who knows? Perhaps he and his wife and their marriage might not have been so very different from the two of us and ours, after all."

This was too much for Martha, but she held her tongue for the rest of the voyage. Inwardly, though, she felt as if Samuel were trying to play some trick on her, lulling her into a false sense of security only to pounce on her again with a new accusation or a new grievance. Even worse was the fact that he seemed to be trying to steal her memories away from her, appropriating the private associations that had made her who she was during the past half century. As she watched his profile out of the corner of her eye, she almost wished for a return to his earlier resentment and vindictiveness. If he continued in this vein, they would both be much happier, but Martha would have somehow lost possession of her own life.

The Houghtons had chosen Ventnor as their ultimate destination, as much for its fame as a haven for Samuel's lungs as for its place in Martha's past. Yet, as if by tacit accord, they avoided any contact with Madeira Road and the legacy of Shelton's Vegetarian Hotel. Instead, they took refuge from the spring storm at a private home near the Undercliff that belonged to a crippled baker whom they'd known since the Great War. This location gave them closer access to the chalk and limestone formations that they both enjoyed walking, and once the rain let up they spent the rest of the day roaming the plateau. By the end of the afternoon, they had viewed the terraces above the beaches and returned to their friend's for a dinner of steaks and homemade bread. The exercise in the brisk air worked marvels on them, and Martha and Samuel slept one of their first untroubled sleeps in weeks.

Most of the next day was given over to idleness. Under a weathered pergola that would soon burst into roses or among grasses soughing on a hillside, the Houghtons sat in comforting silence or wandered without purpose, each glancing about as if in a trance. The sky above them bellied like a sail in the wind that freshened the island with a scent that reminded them impossibly of nutmeg. Martha felt more in her element now, even physically younger, more lithe and clear-skinned, as she pointed out exactly where Aunt Feemy had stood to make some argument about eating meat and where Gandhi had gestured at a grazing bull that was stronger than all of them put together. Such memories nourished her, but her husband, too, participated. Samuel often led her about as a gentle taskmaster, prodding her forward with cues and the beginnings of sentences that he left hanging so that she might finish them. There was nothing intrusive or commanding about his manner. It was only the kind of code that longtime friends always share. At nightfall, the two returned arm in arm, schoolmates on an outing, both of them nodding over the passing sights as if they'd lived on the island all their lives.

This pattern of interwoven past and present held for the remainder of their holiday. In Chichester, at the start of a spell of drier weather, they scouted the area around Alice's house and school, on the lookout for any inquisitive people with notepads or cameras. All seemed safe enough, but then Martha recalled her daughter's guarded manner on the telephone, and a figure in a long coat who later turned out to be a local vicar finally spooked them away. At Samuel's suggestion, they sought shelter in the cathedral. "Let's take a look at the grave of that composer whose music I missed hearing you sing," he said to his wife as he steered her through knots of gawping daytrippers. "Now, why couldn't Rita Venden have made a recording of that?" The interior of the church, with its stony gloom and high ribbed vaulting, proved to be somewhat less welcoming than they might have wished, though Samuel did admire its craftsmanship. As for Martha, she started at every echo, tried to rub her husband's chest warm with her hands, and appeared apologetic that the cathedral was there at all. The tomb of Gustav Holst was somehow a fitting close to their visit, a famous figure whom neither of them had ever known or in any way understood.

At last, after a tour of the coastline, the Houghtons arrived at the Savoy Hotel in London. From here, it was easy for them to renew their slight acquaintance with the city. As in Southampton, only far worse, the mutilations of the war were still evident on all sides — cicatrices of fallen masonry, bus clippies deafened by blasts, man-made craters, and shopkeepers who still wore their A.R.P. uniforms behind their counters. Yet, in the past two and a half years, the legendary stubbornness of Londoners had steadily reasserted itself. The men had returned to their factories and their pints with only the smallest frightened crooks in their necks. The women had found further promise in their work, both inside and outside the home. And the children, most of them looking older than their calendar years, had invented new games of courage and sacrifice. All this was soon revealed to the Houghtons, as they taxied and tubed from one end of the city to the other and gradually came to feel a little less uncomfortable in each other's presence.

Not until their third day in London did Martha realize that her husband had been following a plan all along. Lolloping from one site to the next in his unwieldy overcoat, he had cleverly guided her through an agenda that he must have mapped out in advance. First Portsmouth, then Ventnor and Chichester, and now London — he had, in truth, been retracing Gandhi's visits to England, as far as Martha herself and Rebecca's various publications must have instructed him. A pointless detour through the neighborhood surrounding Notting Hill Gate station finally showed his hand, as Samuel immersed them in a gathering of Indian students with their lilting voices and their blend of vermilion paste and jasmine. Martha felt almost more bemused than offended by the ruse. It seemed that she'd been right from the start. Samuel's earlier enthusiasm for the *Bhagavad Gita* and for the late Indian martyr were only misdirections to hide his true feelings. He hadn't yet really forgiven her at all.

On their last night in the hotel, Martha challenged him with it as he stood creasing his trousers over the back of a chair.

"Are you quite satisfied now?" she asked him.

"Satisfied?"

"That Gandhi and I used to do nothing much more together than any pair of common tourists from Hedge End. That with my temperament and his vow of chastity we were no more lovers than —"

"You and I?" he finished for her.

"Samuel!"

He calmly folded back his half of the counterpane and sat down on one side of the bed. The room at the Savoy was more than they could afford, but he had reserved it as something of a treat. There was a main parlor, where Martha stood packing, and, around a dark wooden pillar, a bed in an alcove surmounted by bookshelves and facing mirrors. In such a layout, Samuel had to lean forward and turn his head to make himself heard, but it also afforded him a chance to hide his face from his wife's direct gaze.

"But that's just it, isn't it, Martha?" he resumed. "You know I've always taken you at your word, in this matter as in all others. And you should also know that the physical acts that lovers do aren't what concern me the most. Oh, they might have," he confessed, "in my younger days, as they do most men. Yet now what bother me more are the moments of casual tenderness, unconscious intimacies, the sort that become second nature between two people after years and years of daily contact. Not to mention the fact that, well, there must have been something special about him that, in your eyes, I've always somehow lacked."

"You should never think such things," Martha entreated her husband. "After all, Gandhi and I certainly never shared a fraction of the time that you and I have. A marriage and a friendship can never be the same, can they? Particularly over such great distances, I don't see how one could ever be compared to the other.

"But there's nothing more bothering you, is there?" she asked, watching him rock uneasily on the edge of the bed. "Are you feeling well enough, Samuel? You're looking a bit pale tonight. Is it indigestion?"

After a long minute of hesitation, he told her. He looked ill and embarrassed as he did so, as if something monstrous or shameful were working its way out of him against his strongest efforts to stop it.

"I was only thinking about Walter," he began. He peered almost fearfully at his wife's feet, unable to raise his eyes any farther.

"Walter?"

"Yes, and how he hadn't any of the same strength that the others had, Alice and Nellie and Paul. And, you see, I've worked out the dates and all, and he was so small and undernourished, and no matter what we tried he just didn't seem to pick up, and I was only wondering," Samuel choked out, "I was only wondering if it might not have been because he had a drop or two of a vegetarian's blood in him."

Martha stood still. Yet it wasn't the insult that made her stop and slowly shake her head. It was the sight and the sound of a good man who had, for the moment, forgotten his better self and spoken rash words that he would have given his life to recall. But now it was too late.

"I know, Samuel," she said, graciously averting her eyes, "that, come morning, you'll see all this in a brighter light. You must just be tired."

"I suppose."

The poor man was shaken, his hands fluttering before him like a pair of trapped wings. He couldn't seem to decide where to look next, as his weathered body shrank beneath the bed's heavy canopy.

"We'll both feel better," Martha promised him, "once we're back in our own home. These holidays are always so trying on us. Sometimes I wonder if they're really worth all the trouble! You lie down and rest now, and I'll be along to join you directly."

As Martha dressed for bed, she asked herself if she had ever loved her husband more than she did tonight. His frailty and doubts had won her over, just as they had so many times before — at the birth of each of their children, for instance, or at each of their children's final leave-taking. It was not so much that she celebrated his faults, but that those same faults helped make him more approachable, more human. This might have been one of the best lessons that her long friendship with Gandhi had taught her, the importance of making up the difference whenever loved ones fall short of expectations.

Yet all of her attempts to put the moment behind them fell

flat. A sudden chill had invaded the room as though none of the windows fit snugly in their frames. Now that her husband had admitted to his worst fears, a certain balance between them that had been achieved over decades of fine adjustments had been tilted awry, nudged out of its true alignment. One of the things that Samuel had learned from all his woodworking around the house was that he could always cut or plane more, but not less. Once a plank had been halved or thinned, the action could never be undone. And tonight, Martha suspected, he had discovered to his sorrow that the same rule applied to marriages, that they never fully recovered from any word or thought that diminished them or warped their original shape. The only solution was to discard the ruined wood and start all over again.

On the train ride back to Hedge End, Martha brooded over what lay ahead for her and Samuel. Was this, then, what the rest of their life together would be, a constant alternation between belief and distrust, between acceptance of each other's failings and blind avoidance of the topic altogether? It occurred to her that she might apply a lesson from her long friendship with Gandhi and its enormous distances and widespread time periods.

After waiting for several days at home, unpacking and settling into their routines again, Martha finally came to a decision. Then she informed Samuel, with as little fanfare or discussion as possible, that in a few weeks' time she would be sailing alone to India.

10

"My word!" cried Nellie, her thickly painted face threatening to crack apart. "How did Father take the news?"

"Not as badly as you might imagine," Martha replied more coolly than she felt. "There's a lot more pluck in that man than I think we sometimes give him credit for."

She and her two daughters were sitting at an outside table of a teashop in Martha's old neighborhood in Portsmouth. It was a clear day with a flower-scented wind and enough warming sun to illuminate the white linen cloth that was set with a teapot, a toast rack, and a jar of marmalade. Martha had invited them to a tour of her past and a final lunch before she finished her preparations prior to leaving for Bombay.

"I still can't believe he didn't make an awful row," Alice put in. "It's not like him to roll over and play dead so easily."

"But what else can a man do," Martha said with a triumphant smile, "once he sees that a woman has made her mind up for good?"

The truth, of course, was far different. Over an everyday breakfast, Samuel had almost exploded, his face reddening to a dangerous purple.

"What the hell do you mean, you're sailing to India? When did you decide all this? And why wasn't I consulted about it or even invited along?"

"Well, if you'd really like to come —"

"You know perfectly well that you're stronger than I am and that I'd never survive the rigors of the voyage, the heat and the spicy foods and all. But damn it, Martha," he'd sputtered. "Here you had me thinking that we'd already laid all this Gandhi rot to rest. I mean to say, we've argued and we've fought over it, we've discussed it and we've talked around it, we've forgiven each other over and over, and I've even tried to meet you halfway by getting to know him and his ideas better. And now here you go again, hauling it all back in between us again. It just isn't fair!"

"But this isn't really about Gandhi, Samuel. It's about his dying son, Harilal. Have you forgotten about him? He's still alone and in need of some friend to comfort him in his final hours. I realize that you don't know him from Adam, no more than I do, but he's still a fellow human being who's suffering and who needs my help."

"Your help?" Her husband had crossed his arms across his chest, always a sure sign that he knew he was in the wrong, but that he would never give in. "What about his own people, his own family, over there? He must have brothers and kids around who can see to him. Why in God's name should he have to drag you around the world to hold his hand when you're more needed by us here? You're hardly a young woman anymore, Martha, and he must know that. It seems like sheer impertinence in him even to suggest it."

"Oh, he hasn't the faintest idea that I'm coming. I thought I'd mentioned that before."

This bit of news had set her husband off even more, until the scuffling of his angry feet on the polished floor had earned him a scowl from his wife.

"I'm sorry. It won't happen again. But listen, Martha," he'd implored her with renewed energy, "this is patently absurd. You're about to sct off on a ten-thousand-mile ocean voyage to see a man who's already tried to extort you through the post, a man who by all accounts has always been the worst of the Gandhi clan, and a man who will most likely be dead and buried —"

"Cremated."

"Dead and cremated, then, long before you even get out of the Suez Canal. It's madness, I tell you, for you even to contemplate such a rash act. The price of the ticket alone would drain our bank account of most of our savings."

"That's why I've taken Philip up on his yearly offer to pay my way to Perth. All the ships stop in Bombay, and I don't see why I can't just jump off one, stay with thc boy for as long as is necessary, and then jump onto another. Then, after a week or two with my brother and his family, I can retrace the route and be home again in time for the autumn harvests. You'll hardly even miss me," Martha had argued, "and anyway we can always keep in touch by letter and wire, can't we?"

In the calm of their kitchen, her arguments had sounded rational enough, but Samuel was still upset that the entire interruption of their married life was not yet over and done with.

"I don't suppose it would do much good for me to forbid you out of hand," he'd partially surrendered. "But I still don't see what you hope to get out of it. What? Adventure?

Time alone away from me and the children? A chance to see the world that I've never been rich enough to show you? Some glimpse of the life that you might have had, but didn't? Sometimes I simply don't understand you, Martha," Samuel had complained from beneath the hand with which he was rubbing his brow. "Why should you ever want to make more trouble for yourself and us than what we've already had?"

It had taken his wife a few minutes of reflection over her tea to come up with an answer.

"I suppose it's because I feel that I haven't finished yet," she'd finally said in a quieter voice. "I started something sixty years ago, and now I have to see it through to the end. You know what it's like when one of your projects at home gets delayed by the weather or illness or a shortage of supplies. You sit around and fume and count the hours, and nothing — absolutely nothing — will do except returning to the task and concluding it to your own satisfaction. That must be the way it is with me. Sixty years ago, by mere chance, I became involved in a set of other lives and other destinies that I've kept up with at intervals ever since. I was like Philip, in a way, the distant relation who's never fully in our thoughts or completely out of them. I wrote, I called, I even met with Gandhi from time to time to give him a sister's or perhaps a mother's advice, and I was always somehow connected to both him and his family. Now," Martha said, sighing, "his murder at the end of January has robbed me of all that before I even had the chance to finish it. And I don't think I can bear that, Samuel. I just don't think I can. Not for very much longer.

"You say it's the life that I might have had, but didn't," she'd concluded while Samuel had turned his face toward the window. "But I say it's an integral part of the life that I've always had, yet never really acknowledged. And now I think it's time that I did."

Weeks later, seated with her two daughters at the teashop, Martha revealed nothing of this conversation, but only went on, "Besides, your father knows that I'm badly in need of a change, what with all the publicity and his own constant grousing that I've been enduring lately. He said that things will never be the same between us if I go. But I said that things will never be the same between us whether I go or don't go. He's just going to have to accustom himself to what I feel I have to do. Or not!" she added, mostly to see the astonishment register on her daughters' innocent faces.

Martha sat back to view them better. In appearance, they were not so much alike. Alice was strict in profile, dry and underfed, not entirely free of twitches as she sat stiff in a steel-colored suit. She wore glasses, but they didn't seem to help her out here in the open air, for she kept staring from side to side as if she'd suddenly awakened from sleepwalking and wondered where she was. Never fully at ease in public, she was too conscious of her empty hands and crossed and uncrossed them in front of her. Anyone seeing her could guess, even before she spoke, that her voice would be too level, too graceless, to inspire anything more in her students than dutiful respect. Still, for all her sternness, there were times when her nervous, sidelong glances became pathetically timid, like those of a small girl lost at twilight and searching for her way home.

Her sister, on the other hand, though almost an opposite, was hardly more distinctive. Nellie was heavier, ruddier, and far better dressed in softer fabrics and colors, the kind that after a suitable delay were borrowed from the pages of magazines and newspapers. Yet on her rounder, slacker body the clothes hung crookedly, as they would have had they fallen already arranged out of an upstairs window onto a housewife returning from the grocer's. Frowsy even in her sophistication, Nellie had grown gray in her efforts to construct a world in which husbands didn't misplace their affections and sons didn't perish overseas. Sitting together as they were at the table, slightly apart from each other, the two sisters might have been taken for absolute strangers. But the truth was that the late war's losses had changed them both profoundly until, whether they themselves were aware of it or not, they were becoming more similar by the hour. Alice had begun to prettify her flat in Chichester and herself as well during the singles' Saturday nights at her local community center, while Nellie had started volunteering her spare time at a charity orphanage. Neither suspected the other's inner transformation, nor did their mother, but before long both sisters were to have some dramatic surprises in store for those who loved them.

"But India!" Nellie continued to object. "India! You can't be serious."

"Didn't I tell you" — Martha bent forward eagerly — "that I've received a third letter from Bombay?"

"No! What's this one got to say for itself?" wondered Alice.

"Well, it seems the unhappy fellow hasn't much time left. I can almost hear the suffering in his written words, the same sort of bereavement and regret that I've been feeling myself. All he says he wants now is to be forgiven, only the one he wants forgiveness from the most is beyond his reach. Perhaps," Martha suggested, "it's I who can bring him what he wants and needs so badly."

"Still, I'm afraid I have to agree with Nellie," Alice forced herself to say, "and advise you against this. A trip to India at your age could prove disastrous. The heat and the dysentery and the Hindu-Muslim violence alone would be too much for you. You'd never even make it all the way to Uncle Philip's, much less all the way back here."

"But —"

"No, no," the two sisters insisted as one.

Nellie went on, "We'll hear no more about this foolishness, thank you. It's our responsibility to look after you and make life easier for you and, when the time comes, be beside you in your last moments."

And Alice concluded, "What kind of daughters would we be — and what kind of a son would Paul be — if we didn't do the same for you as you and Father did for us when we were all small and helpless?"

Taken somewhat aback by her daughters' show of devotion, Martha sat silent for a while, stirring the last of her tea and gazing at the mobile pattern of the marmalade jar's crystal shadow in the daylight. She followed its course over the cloth's wrinkles and under the teapot's spout, studying it as carefully as a beekeeper would the meaningful dance of a bee. At last, when the reflections came to a standstill against her handbag, she raised her head and regarded her two daughters again.

"I'm afraid, my dears, that you're both a mite confused about the situation here." She sat up straighter, and during the remainder of her speech her stooped back grew straighter still. "I'm not asking for your permission or even for your blessing. I'm telling you what I intend to do. As much as I love all you children, and as much as I'll miss you while I'm away, you have to understand that I'm not yours to pamper and protect. I'm your mother, yes, but I'm also myself. I may be old," she reminded them lightly, yet with a serious undertone, "but I'm first and foremost still an adult with all an adult's rights and needs and wishes. Just because I seem to be shrinking down to the size of a child doesn't mean I am one!"

"Oh, Martha," Nellie interposed, "we know all that. But —"

"And I think it's vitally important for me to make my own way in the world, at least in this one matter. I believe it will help build my character and save me from falling into error again. No," she told them firmly, "it's time for me to act my age and take better charge of my own heart and mind. And it's time for you, girls, to do the same for yourselves, not for me. Let's please not make the mistake of trying to live everyone else's life instead of our own."

After a fourth pot of tea and some sweet cakes, and after more talk and promises, Martha and her daughters finally came to an accord that satisfied them all. Martha would be careful and stay in touch, Alice would visit her sister and her nieces and nephews more frequently, and Nellie would now and again leave her household to its own devices. And they would both look after Samuel as much as he would let them in his wife's absence. In this manner, each of them hoped to retain her independence without feeling too unbearably alone.

On the station platform, all three women bade one another farewell and promised to have more such teas together again soon. Then they each caught their separate trains to go home.

As if to foreshadow the journey ahead, the surface of the P and O quay in Tilbury was so awash with travelers that it rocked like a sea. Nearly a thousand or more stood and swayed in the blue May morning, caught between staying and leaving as between sleeping and waking. The majority of them were Irish emigrants whose fares had been paid by the Australian government so they might move there to live and work, populate inhuman landscapes, and in most senses disappear. The men and women on the leading edge of the throng had less time for goodbyes, for all their thoughts were on the ship rising above them. The *Ranchi* had been one of a quartet — including also the *Ranpura,* the *Rawalpindi,* and the *Rajputana* — that, before the war, had been the stars of the Peninsular and Oriental Steam Navigation Company's London-to-Bombay run. The last named, as a matter of fact, had transported Gandhi himself to the Round Table Conference in London in 1931. But the ship docked at Tilbury today was the only one of the four that had survived the conflict intact, and even its glories had visibly faded. Gone were the second of its funnels, the yellow gleams in its railings and decks, the snap of its pennants, even the jut of its bow. Now it squatted low and gurgled like a frog and with every added family seemed to sink unhealthily into its floating pools of oil.

Unfazed by all the activity, Martha doggedly made her way with her single valise past the pursers until she reached the uppermost level of the ship, where her momentum finally failed her and she stood staring down undecided at the ticket in her hand.

That was where the young navigator of the *Ranchi* found her as he was making his last-minute rounds.

"May I help you, madam?" he asked her with a touch to his cap.

"Perhaps you can. I have a reserved berth somewhere —"

"Ah," he exclaimed, reaching out for her ticket, "one of our paying guests. There aren't that many of you, this time out."

"But it's marked POSH at the bottom, and I really didn't mean to travel so expensively. I certainly hope," she added with a deferential nod at the hundreds of Irish below, "that I'm not putting anyone else out, especially one of the children."

"Not at all." He smiled broadly at her and lowered his voice. "I think someone in the office was only having you on a bit, Mrs. —"

"Houghton."

"Mrs. Houghton. Dennis Biggs, ship's navigator, at your service. No," he went on, "this designation means nothing special. It's only an old reference to which side of the ship gets less sun and is therefore cooler. Do you see?" He pointed at the acronym. "It simply means 'port out, starboard home,' or on the left-hand side of the ship on the way down to India and on the right-hand side on the way back. We don't use it much anymore, not with all the updated facilities that we have on board. But they do say that's how we came by the word 'posh' itself, though I can't imagine any of the dictionary makers looking to the P and O for their inspiration."

The young man was brisk and friendly, high-colored by so much sun and sea, boyishly overjoyed to be able to play at sailor every day. He stood tall over Martha and gave her, by means of his matter-of-fact tone and easy manner, some portion of the confidence that she lacked.

"This is my first trip out," she explained as he led her toward her quarters, "my first trip anywhere, actually. And I've never been on the open ocean, no more than to the Isle of Wight and back. I can already feel that this unsteadiness beneath the feet is something that will take getting used to."

"You'll have your sea legs before you know it," the navigator assured her.

Martha rambled on, more to herself than to her new friend, "A woman my age probably has no business going anywhere, least of all halfway around the globe. But, when you suddenly find yourself at odds with everyone around you, even your loved ones, you can get some terribly dark notions running about inside your head. At such times, you hardly know which way to turn, until you finally choose the maddest option available to you."

By now, as decent a sort as the young man was, Biggs had reverted to his usual workday demeanor and agreed with the old woman perhaps more mechanically than he meant to. At her door, he handed back her ticket and gave a fractional bow as he gestured her in. He wished her a happy voyage and promised her that, whatever was taking her to India, the experience would be unforgettable.

Once the *Ranchi* had got under way and out into the roadstead, the emigrants settled in for a sweltering, lurching journey that would take the better part of a month. They crammed themselves beyond capacity into cabins, strolled the decks incessantly for air, and before long set up smoking spirit lamps to brew unofficial cups of tea for seasick mothers and toddlers just off the breast. Opposite Southampton, Martha watched her own home shrinking away behind her from a sheltered alcove in the stern. The view of the shoreline, wrinkling in the mist, tore at her. How long would it be, she wondered, before she saw it again? She was almost seventy-three now, and Gandhi's death at seventy-eight, although unnatural, had reminded her how close she was to the end. From such a distance, she couldn't make out Hedge End, but she could picture what Samuel was doing in their home: the same things he always did, putter about, read his motor journals, shuffle holes through his slippers, and retreat to the sanctum of his toolshed. Martha had often fantasized about burning the blasted thing to the ground, if only to reclaim all of her husband's hours that it had stolen away from her over the years. Yet now, though she had steeled herself against missing him, she began to doubt her decision and wished that she hadn't been so unyielding against Samuel's cautions and demands. All her brave talk upon leaving him and her children now seemed to have been mainly bluster. The imagined sight of her husband fumbling arthritically over his own meal preparations reminded her of how much she treasured even his most irritating shortcomings.

As the coast slipped farther and farther away and the *Ranchi* swung heavily toward the Continent, Martha also finally let herself acknowledge the reality of Gandhi's death. What worried her most was how it must have felt to him. If only it had been too sudden for any thoughts or feelings whatsoever! Then, perhaps, she could endure the loss. For a moment, all the lessons that Gandhi had tried to teach her about rebirth and the greater soul came back to her, and she grew excited at the prospect of his continuing on somehow, perhaps even now and even here. She fancied that she could see him down on deck as one of the little Irish boys whose clothes didn't reach his wrists or ankles, pantomiming sailing or piracy, yet with a favorite gingham sleepmate sticking out of his pocket. But then Martha's common sense returned, and she stared dully out at the furrows in the ocean as they were crushed flat beneath the hull.

For the first few days, she kept to her cabin, as much for privacy as because of nausea. She took her meals alone, walked the decks only when most of the other passengers were sleeping, and avoided the negligible activities that the ship offered. Yet, somewhere between Lisbon and Gibraltar, a change occurred. There were, as Biggs had told her, very few paying customers on this trip. Affordable air travel was fast approaching, and the steamship companies had to scramble to make up for all their losses during the past decade. Supplying Australia with new settlers soon became even more profitable for them than repatriating exiles or delivering war brides. To complement all the farmers, laborers, and tradespeople, some professionals were needed as well, teachers and fresh doctors who were willing to work under the most challenging conditions. The other travelers on the first-class level were few in number — a spindly teacher from Exeter with his family; a disheveled, chain-smoking doctor with mismatched socks; an Indian scholar returning home; a timber merchant with a limp and a wife; a trio of brothers who might as easily have been Laplanders as Londoners; and a very dark man in a very white suit whom Martha took to be an Australian aboriginal. But each of these companions eventually held his own fascination for her, and she began to talk and dine with them accordingly.

Yet it was the hundreds of Irish emigrants over whom she marveled the most. The navigator had informed her that the *Ranchi* was designed to hold six hundred and that now she was carrying closer to nine. This made for a crowding on the lower decks that was almost tidal in nature. Masses of caps and kerchiefs moved from end to end or from side to side like the rippling under a snake's skin, bearing all along with them. The course of an occasional bright scarf or raised hand could be charted as clearly as the ship's own until it was overwhelmed. But in spite of the tight quarters, the settlers kept up their spirits and lent their part of the ship all the holiday mood of a theater or a street fair.

Not all of the paying guests, however, regarded them as charitably. The doctor was of the opinion that such overloading was hazardous to the vessel, not to mention illegal, and a breeding ground for contagions that, out of compassion for the ladies present, he refused to specify.

"Oh, rest assured," he pronounced over one of the open-air tables with a wave of his cigar to ward off midges, "that we shall think ourselves fortunate to see Bombay by the first of June, and Fremantle who knows how long after that. I've made this run too many times before not to know what sort of troubles to expect."

"Troubles?" asked someone.

"Well, the gross tonnage of this ship, you see, is just under sixteen thousand, six hundred, and fifty, and its average speed seventeen knots. Now" — he calculated in the air — "we add three hundred excess passengers and factor in all their accompanying baggage and belongings, and you can begin to see the potential for difficulties. Most of these folks are moving for life, remember, and have whole housefuls of effects riding down in the holds."

"You don't really think they'd let us founder, do you?" the teacher worried.

"It's not the weight or the capacity that concern me so much as the time, the possible delays." The doctor frowned importantly. "If we should happen to slow down or stick in the Suez Canal — a not unheard-of phenomenon with these old wrecks — then we expose ourselves to a harsh, foul atmosphere that might start an epidemic among us, especially one coming up from below."

"Still," the timber merchant observed, with a nod directed over the near railing, "they'll probably lose a few en route, as they always do. You can't cheat statistics."

"But they'll add some, too." His wife's voice was birdlike, and she always wore yellow. "I've seen many of the girls who look as if they might deliver in a matter of weeks or even days."

"Correct, madam." The doctor looked appreciatively at the woman sitting across from him and sighed. "They have some of their own physicians and midwives down there, of course. But there's no doubt that my skills will be required some time before this crossing is done and that I shall have to miss my sleep — again! An occupational hazard," he boasted with a suggestive leer that was entirely lost upon the timber merchant's wife.

"You mentioned Bombay," one of the brothers from London — Wapping, to be precise — spoke up. "For how long do we put in there? Does anyone know? I only ask," he hurried on, "because of the possibility of civil unrest. It's been no more than four months since Gandhi was killed, and then there was all that partitioning trouble already. How much danger are we going to be putting ourselves in, merely by calling at the port?"

Martha, whose attention had been wandering toward the brown Iberian peninsula passing by, now turned her better ear toward the talk.

"The P and O uses the Mazagon Dock," the doctor reflected, "and I've never known it to be overrun by ruffians. I think, even with most of the British leaving the city, the authorities will keep everything well in check. They shouldn't want to lose all our business, not when their economy is so uncertain on its own." And his telling smirk let the others know just how vital their contributions were to the world's welfare. They couldn't reach Australia soon enough for him, he declared, where there was at least some minimal degree of civilization.

Bristling, Martha was about to disagree, when the eavesdropping Indian scholar at the next table pulled his chair over to join them.

"Oh, pardon me, but our civilization is old, very old," he said in a bright, crisp accent. "And most advanced. Don't believe, please, everything you read in the European newspapers about us. Even with all our current upset, the land and its people are most beautiful and peaceable and eager to be your friends."

Everyone mumbled polite pleasantries and introduced himself. When her turn came, Martha made it a point to extend her warmest welcome to the man who reminded her so much of a youthful Gandhi. Dr. R. K. Rao — "No, no, you would have no hope of pronouncing those awful given names of mine!" — was in his thirties but might have passed for ten years younger or older. He had a round, loam-tinted face beneath a riot of black hair, the most brilliant teeth that had ever been seen in England, a compact torso grown hungry in libraries, and a girl's feet. He was a professor at some Indian university whose name no one quite caught, specializing in the history of his nation's philosophies and religions. His brief description of Sanskrit alone was so infectious that he was soon requested to scribble out a few words of its Devanagari script on the damp wood before him.

"Lovely, isn't it?" he implored them. "And surprisingly close to your own language. Did you know that we share many words, for example 'brother' and '*bhratar*'? Surely this must mean that we are none of us so very different."

Martha agreed with him enthusiastically, though the others at the table exchanged reserved looks. The professor didn't let this reception deter him from chittering gaily on about all the things he was certain that he and his traveling companions had in common.

"Even in our religions," he cried out to the circle of stiff smiles, "we are not very far apart at all! We Hindus have but one God, though we call him by many names. And, when we finally die after all our countless lives, we hope to be brought close into the presence of God. Isn't that what your heaven is, too? The soul at last in the company of the Soul from which it came?"

The teacher was the first to object. "But we have the Trinity or, in some cases, the Virgin Mary —"

"As we have our Trimurti and our Krishna and, more recently, our lost Gandhiji, our Mahatma! Even our Buddhists — the ones we used to have, no, we have very few of them left to us now — even our Buddhists teach us that the source of all suffering is separation, the unreal Self distinguishing itself from all others. This has forever been at the root of all the world's troubles, even the Western world's," Rao pleaded with outstretched hands. "The failure of brother to recognize brother, sister sister."

This lecture provoked a lengthy debate about race, morality, and politics in which even the Australian aborigine participated. Most of the paying passengers soon came to accept the Indian scholar's presence among them, though they still found both his speech and his arguments outlandish. Martha herself sat back in silence, as if the better to study him and listen.

"I tell you, though," Rao interrupted the others, "when we do finally reach Bombay, we must — but for how long does the *Ranchi* stop there?" he asked the doctor.

"That depends on when we arrive. No more than a day or two, I should say."

"A pity. So you who are to go on must keep yourselves, as your Epictetus so wisely teaches us, always within earshot of the ship." No one else recognized the allusion, so he pressed on. "But, as I meant to say, we simply must make a visit to the Elephanta Caves, all of us, all together, no more than an hour's launch ride from the city. They are sublime!" he crowed with a roll of his eyes. "Magnificent statues of Siva and Parvati and the demons Andhaka and Ravana, wonderful pillars and halls, and plenty of places inside and out to picnic. The entire Gharapuri island offers endless curiosities. Listen to me now, I am about to enumerate them for you."

It must have been the philosopher's nervous excitement at

finding himself facing so many foreigners that made him monopolize the conversation in a way that, in a more self-conscious man, might have appeared rude. But Rao's squeaking voice and inability to sit still seemed to disarm his listeners and make them forgive in him what they would have never forgiven in one another. Indeed, they looked upon him as a newborn or a pet, something inoffensive and amusing to help them while away the time. The Australian aborigine followed his clothing rather than his skin and joined forces with the British passengers against the outsider. But, though there was more than a little condescension in their shared attitude, so far it hadn't degenerated into frozen civility or brute malice.

As evening fell, the group at the table dispersed in a pale imitation of the more massive Irish scattering below. Martha remained behind, refusing two or three offers of sherry or a stroll about the decks. She wanted, she said, to meditate on the night sea, and on herself. Now in the shadow of a hanging lifeboat, she silently wondered what on earth she was doing here. Was she really answering the call of an old friend's dying son or merely escaping? If the latter, then escaping from what? She thought she knew — from a small village with too much idle time on its hands and too many snooping eyes, from a husband who couldn't understand a part of her life that he hadn't shared in, from her own future, which, without Gandhi, promised to be short, uneventful, monotonous, and soulless. That, Martha realized as she watched a crop of stars that seemed to rise and fall independently of the ship, was the basic difference between Samuel and Mohandas. Her husband was earthy, good, and commonsensical, a man for whom the modern, mechanical world held no mysteries. Yet Gandhi had introduced her to another, older world, that of the spirit and of much grander mysteries, and had made her feel infinite in scope, almost immortal. How could she now be satisfied with anything less?

As for Harilal Gandhi, she thought as she got up to leave, the poor boy would probably be dead long before she reached him, or as good as, and she would be stranded in a strange, unruly city with nothing to do but wait for the next ship to take her first to Philip's and then back home. But how much of a home would she have to go back to, with everything so greatly and forever changed?

II

Yet, in the morning, the Mediterranean sparkled and widened. Bluer, calmer, with cleaner and more perfumed winds, the enclosed sea spread out before Martha like a turquoise lawn at sunrise. An infectious frivolity took possession of the ship, as the warmth of the south combined with a hint of African spices to remind the passengers that they had left their former routines far behind. Even the faint-hearted teacher from Exeter asked Martha a few days later with a shiver of anticipation what she intended to do during their stop at Marseilles.

"I myself," Carroll Sharpe whispered confidentially, "should like to buy my wife and daughter a little something to remember our journey by. I think that's so important in a family, don't you, those casual acts of thoughtfulness?"

"Oh, I do." Martha reached out to steady herself on a railing as the ship churned its way toward the southernmost edge of France. "My husband surprises me all the time with flowers or biscuits or some silly doodad that he's made me on the sly in his workshop. I wouldn't give up any of them for worlds."

"You must miss him terribly."

"Of course I do. But do you know what it is?" she said to him. "Sometimes I think that there's really not much more to life than loss. I mean, when you get to my age, you find soon enough that — even after you've taken into account all the marvels and joys that offset all the horrors and tears — the whole balanced affair is actually rather sad, isn't it? I doubt if it could ever be otherwise," Martha added as she came to a halt beneath the ship's vibrating funnel. "Defeat seems to be grown into the very marrow of our days."

Startled by her bleak manner, Sharpe inquired after her plans. Did she mean to go ashore tomorrow? Sightsee a bit? Shop?

"Plans?" Martha suddenly cried out in what sounded almost like anger. "But that's just what I've been trying to tell you all along, my dear man. I haven't a clue *what* I'm going to do next!"

To calm her down, the teacher insisted that she accompany him through the port streets of Marseilles while his wife stayed behind with their daughter, who was confined to their cabin with the flu. The day they spent together among the wide-trousered sailors and vendors frying *socca* pancakes under dangling cigarettes did them both good. Martha accused herself of being a frightful biddy and a sobersides, and Carroll Sharpe scoffed both labels aside at once. He, in turn, would have never chanced a bowl of steaming shellfish, if his new friend hadn't gently bullied him into it. By the end of the afternoon, as if they'd been related to each other all their lives, Martha and the young man who reminded her so much of Paul formed an inseparable pair.

Their bond continued and grew across the Mediterranean. The *Ranchi* skirted Italy and Greece and dodged the various islands as it sailed determinedly for Port Said and the bronze statue of Ferdinand de Lesseps gesturing toward his Suez Canal. All the way, from elevated bow to awninged stern, alone together or with little Charlotte between them — now it was the mother's turn to lie sick in bed — Martha and the teacher from Exeter seemed to hold each other upright through the middle part of the journey. At Naples and Malta, they ate squid beneath hanging fishing nets and visited the brown stone prow of Fort St. Elmo. When one of the ship's twin screws unhinged at Piraeus, Martha and the Sharpes joined the doctor, the timber merchant, and his wife on a three-day walking tour of Athens that, for a time, succeeded in making Martha forget why she had come. The coastline of Egypt was upon them before they knew it, where the heightened yellows of sand and sun burned all other thoughts out of their minds. The passengers, both above and below, stood clustered as one at the bow of the ship, shielding their eyes from the glare, and watched as a landscape older than time hove into view. The general excitement was building.

Then, just as the doctor had foretold, the *Ranchi* soon became hopelessly stalled in the canal, dropping anchor and mooring just above Deversoir, dead in the dead water, and effectively corking the entrance into the Great Bitter Lake. Now it was well past three o'clock in the afternoon, and since seven this morning a thunderous clanging had been heard rising from the engine room. Still the ship refused to budge. Bumboats connected by cables with baskets and pontoon walkways had attached themselves to her flanks like barnacles, allowing the local farmers to peddle their wares and some of the Irish to step off and stretch their legs. It had proved to be a very long day, numb with heat and mists of stinging insects, tense with the frustration of travelers who wanted only to be on their way. The paying guests had tried to make the best of a bad job by playing card games, writing letters home, the women trading recipes and the men exaggerating business triumphs. But, before long, the sluggish atmosphere had seeped into their bones and saturated their willpower, until now even the little Sharpe girl sat as listless as a weed in a sagging deck chair.

Martha and the timber merchant's wife tried to relax in what passed for the coolest part of the ship, a lower deck aft that was shaded by a slatted ceiling and a flapping dewlap of canvas. They were more or less alone, as much as anyone could be in the presence of hundreds of families who had been living in confinement for weeks. The side of the ship gulped loudly against the reinforced bank, as the current strove helplessly against its grounded anchor.

"Well, I certainly thought they'd do righter by us than this." The quiet woman named Hetta exhaled wearily. "If I'd known our pace was going to be this slow, I'd have brought my husband's waders."

Martha needed a moment to appreciate the other's sense of humor, but once she did she warmed to her at once. "Do you and he make such long voyages often?"

"Oh, Lord, do we! I can't tell you how many places we've visited in the past thirty-one years. Africa, Argentina, Borneo, China — my word! do I have these alphabetized? — and now Colombo." She clucked her tongue in exasperation, but there was a glint of even-tempered serenity in her look. "Have you ever stopped to think how much wood the world uses, day in and day out? Why, the paper loss in my own correspondence alone fairly boggles the mind! Sometimes I wonder if that wasn't why Freddie married me as straight off as he did. Only to keep a closer count of his increasing fortunes."

Hetta was one of those women who, in the company of

her husband or other men, wilted into merely echoing the voices she heard around her. But, among her own, she bloomed with wit and intelligence and a tough optimism that surprised Martha and made her wish she'd known her for years.

Hetta Cann appeared perfectly civilized in her light yellow silk jacket and dress, but over one ear she had positioned a sedge flower swept up out of one of the marshes bordering the canal. Such gestures might have seemed affected in a woman in her mid-fifties, but she wore her age exceptionally well, her rouged cheeks and sculpted eyebrows making her look a third younger than she was. At the same time, there was enough gravity in her firm, small mouth that even someone of Martha's generation was made to feel welcomed and understood.

"But the adventures you must have had!" cried Martha in envy. "This is my first time anywhere so far from home, and I'm fully carried away by it all."

"It's true, it's true, we have rather made the most of it." Hetta offered Martha a cigarette, gasped at her refusal, then greedily lit one for herself. She smoked with her head slightly lowered, as if to hide the act from prying eyes. "Still," she went on with a look at the surrounding sand, "after a while one begins to pine for immobility, if you see what I mean. Not this kind exactly, but the other. You know, a place that's one's own for two years running, a pause to all the suitcases and trains and ships like this one, and please God no more treks through forests with tigers or elephants tramping alongside. Do you see those scars on my ankles?" she asked, propping one heel atop a toe. "That, my friend, is what you get when you forget where you are and dress for the Strand in the midst of Malaysia."

"Do you share so much, then, in Mr. Cann's trade?"

"Well, I do and I don't. Personally, I couldn't tell a teak from a tea tree without a manual. I leave all that to him. Where I do come in," she said, sitting forward, "is in the area of finances and public relations. Poor Freddie couldn't balance an account book to save his life, and when it comes to dealing with landowners and diplomats and the like he only stutters and balks. All he knows is wood, the grain of it, the feel, and even the smell of it. But we're not just buying and selling trees, I always tell him. We're changing people's lives, either for good or ill, and that's what he seems to have such a hard time remembering." A sweep as from a soaring cloud — but here there were no clouds — darkened Hetta's features, yet she soon recovered and carelessly tossed her cigarette over the railing. "I cherish my husband deeply," she concluded, "as I'm sure you do yours, but sometimes they have to be reminded of how important people are. Our own people, their people, others — it doesn't really matter. None of us can live in this world as if we were the only ones in it. As Auden put it at the start of the war, 'We must love one another or die.' It's as simple as that."

The two women talked for over an hour about their respective lives and families, while behind them a straggle of fuming ships continued to unwind. They rested together, cooled off, had their evening meals brought up from the galley, laughed at a lone ibis stalking through the shallows, and grew satisfied even with the delay. Finally, as an almost icy blue night descended upon the canal, the chain of riding lights on the water fell asleep, and most of the voices on board became anonymous enough to be confessional, to a degree.

"I'm going to Bombay first to see the son of a friend," Martha admitted without mentioning any names. "He's sick, dying most likely, and alone, and I thought he deserved not to be, now at his end, the same as everyone else. To be honest with you, though, I really haven't the foggiest notion what I'm doing, or whether it's the right thing to do, or whom I might be injuring, or what to do after." Her chair creaked with indecision as she added, "My mind's been in such a spin lately that I hardly know where I am. And now, with the children too rightly busy with their own lives and my husband and I growing further and further apart, I find myself at loose ends. I swear, this is the first time in all my days, I think, that I have absolutely no idea what might happen to me tomorrow."

"Liberating, isn't it?" Hetta interjected.

"Excuse me? Well, I suppose it might be, for some." Martha seemed to ponder for a moment, then she resumed tentatively, "The fact of the matter is, you see, the dying Indian's father and I were — close. And my husband's found out about it, and it's upset him far beyond all sensible bounds. And I was just wondering," she finished in a single, tumbling breath, "if you'd ever had such a friendship in all your travels and if you felt that it was at all a proper thing for a married woman to have and —"

Hetta hurried to assure Martha that it was, that over the years she herself had made numerous acquaintances who were as dear to her as her own dear husband, only in profoundly different ways.

"A woman's heart," she postulated, "has more chambers in it than the four the doctors would have us believe. A man's also, I don't doubt. I shouldn't worry too much about it if I were you. Love can take so many forms that even I haven't neared the end of counting them, and life has its own sublime way of working these things out. I'm sure your man understands that," she comforted Martha, "even if he doesn't yet know that he does. Have you had any wires or letters from him?"

"No, I haven't, only a couple from my son and one of my daughters. They say he's doing fine on his own, which I'm not sure if I should be happy or unhappy about. I always thought he needed me more than that, but now I'm beginning to wonder. It's unsettling, don't you think, to find that your life isn't as important as you thought it was, not even to those you thought have known you best?"

"I'll tell you what you should do." Hetta sat up and commanded her: "You should go and consult with Dr. Rao, that Indian fellow in the cabin down the hall from yours. He's amazingly wise. Just the other day, he —

"Hello!" she suddenly interrupted herself. "Did you hear that? Do you feel that?" A deep-rooted shudder moved the entire night around them. "I do think the engines have started up again. Yes, yes, we're definitely off again! Can you believe it? Now if we can only reach the open sea once more."

In the days to come, Martha followed Hetta's advice and began to spend more and more of her time in Dr. Rao's company. At first, he appeared too busy to be bothered. For him, as for all the passengers, the port of Aden proved to be an exhausting rest after the canal and the long, flat doze of the Red Sea. Once they'd put in for a brief stop there, where the temperature was such that one's rubber soles gummed to the deck, the *Ranchi* struck northeastward into a blue sea and sky that were indistinguishable at the horizon. This last part of the voyage wrought the philosopher into such a state of preparation that he might be seen at any hour of the day, stuffing books into boxes, exchanging his Westernized outfits for more traditional garb, and collating the notes of his studies at Oxford. His usual animation deserted him as he set about trying to justify the expenses that his year in England had cost his family and university back in India. He even went to the extreme of offering to sell some of his most cherished volumes in the hope that his illiterate uncle shouldn't think him too altered by his exposure to the outside world. In all this, Martha couldn't help but see the ghost of a young Gandhi long ago, also flustered by change and struggling to ease his transition back into a world that he had almost forgotten.

One evening, when the moon flew smooth above its wrinkled twin, the professor happened to greet Martha where she sat near the forward gunwale and would have continued on, if she hadn't called out after him.

"It looks so much closer from here, doesn't it?"

"India, madam?" he said, turning back politely.

"No, the night sky. Don't you think the stars and the moon look considerably larger at this latitude? I wonder why that should be."

His smile gleamed across at her. "It is because we are here in the very suburbs of heaven," he proclaimed, "or so some of our religious classics tell us. May I?"

"Please do."

Martha made room for him on the bench, and they leaned back together to contemplate the inverted phosphorescent ocean of stars above them and the infinite dark spaces below.

"And what is it that is taking you down to Australia, if one may be so bold as to ask?" Dr. Rao inquired conversationally. "Family? Work? Retirement?"

"Oh, but I stop in Bombay, at least for a good while. Didn't you know?"

"You don't tell me? How perfectly marvelous for you!" He hesitated, then went on, "I trust, though, that you'll have someone waiting to meet you there. If not, you might have difficulty."

After the standard amount of prevarication, Martha finally let him in on the truth about her journey. And it comforted her no end that, of the few people she'd told about her friendship with Gandhi, Rao was the only one who found it to be totally natural and commonplace.

"Ah, the whole world knew Bapuji, did it not?" He nodded as if the martyr's fame had somehow made him physically gigantic. "I spent some time with him myself during his house arrest in the Aga Khan's palace in Poona near Bombay. He was a saint, of course, but a human one, and that must have been why he appealed to so many different people across the boards, as you English say."

"You knew him when he was imprisoned there?" Martha repeated. "That was where his wife died, wasn't it? Some four years ago?"

"Yes, sad, sad." The Indian gazed up at a light falling across the sky and remembered. "Ba, as she was called, I can see her now, as frail as a stick and with sunken cheeks that made her chin look as prominent as a helmet strap. She had heart trouble, did you know, and was forever short of breath with bronchial pneumonia and blue lips and had to sleep sitting up with her head cradled on a table across her bed like a *sadhu* doing penance. It is said that Gandhi kept that table with him to the very end."

"It must have been an affecting scene. Her death there, I mean."

"Terrible. We were all most moved by it."

"Especially her husband," Martha prompted him.

"Really, it was my first sight of him, so I had nothing else to judge by," Dr. Rao observed. "Still, as far as that goes, I don't think I've ever witnessed such sorrow — not outward, you understand — but inward. The poor man was devastated, laid horribly low. She died on his lap, and afterwards he sat alone under a tree, a banyan or a peepul, I forget which, and watched her pyre burn as if his last strength were spent. I only hope," he said and sighed, "that, when my own final moment comes, as much love is shown in my name for everyone to see."

The professor wore wire spectacles that were not unlike Gandhi's, circular goggles that hooked over the ears and gave him the appearance of a myopic clerk. Now these reflected and doubled the silver moon overhead and left Martha wondering if Dr. Rao were more disturbed or exhilarated by the prospect of dying.

"Not to mention the children," she interposed. "I'm sure we should all want our children to be with us at that time."

"Yes, I have two daughters myself."

"And Gandhi — Mrs. Gandhi, that is. Were any of her four sons present at her death?"

Dr. Rao considered for a while, then replied, "They were, three were, I think, now that you remind me. Manilal was in South Africa just then, but Devadas and Ramdas were there. And, later, Harilal — though, my goodness, how much better it would have been for all concerned had he not!"

By maintaining a silence, Martha was able to induce him to tell her the rest of the story, details that she'd never been able to pry out of Gandhi in his letters.

"Well, they had a demon's own time of it, you know, finding him," Dr. Rao continued, reminiscing in the dark. "He'd taken to running with bad seeds, and they had to scour the entire slums of Poona just to bring him in to his mother. And then he was as drunk as a bishop to boot, so much so that he started up some pains in the dear woman's chest and they had to bundle him out again. Harilal had always been a source of woe to his parents with all his impossible business schemes and his temporary conversion to Islam and his rebellious nature. His troubles, I suppose, dated back to the death of his wife in the great influenza epidemic of 'eighteen and of his son, Rasik, from typhoid a decade later, though I must say his father certainly handled both of his own similar tragedies far better than he."

"Some people are simply weaker or more sensitive than others," Martha theorized, "through no fault of their own."

"True. At any rate, Harilal's daughter came in to see the old lady the next day with her uncle Devadas, and that good man promised to look after his wastrel brother's children as well as he could." With a troubled clearing of the throat, the Indian added, "They say that Harilal himself was present at his father's funeral at Rajghat, but that he was drunk again and so chose to go unrecognized in the multitude. After that, he disappeared as completely as the Mahatma's ashes into the holy Ganges — until now, of course, if he really is at some hospital in Bombay, waiting for you. But it's a wonder, isn't it, all the strange ways that love can take among us in this world?"

Martha, now at the ship's railing, kept her own counsel, remarking only that there was no accounting for its mysteries.

This comment sparked in the professor a disquisition on the various categories of human love. Dr. Rao, it turned out, was a devotee of the god Siva and was particularly fond of the Virasaiva poet-saints of the tenth to the twelfth centuries. One of these was a woman, Mahadevi by name, who adhered to the three traditional Sanskrit classifications of love — love forbidden, love in separation, and love in union. "'The heart in misery,'" he quoted passionately in a thin falsetto, "'has turned upside down! The blowing gentle breeze is on fire! O friend moonlight burns like the sun!'"

Martha responded to his growing inspiration and thought she could detect in her own life a similar three-part arrangement. The forbidden, the separated, and the unified seemed to fit her love for both Gandhi and Samuel, only in different ways and to varying degrees. Where all of that left her now, though, was more than she could fathom.

"But I've upset you now, haven't I, madam, with all my versifying?" Dr. Rao apologized as he came up to join her at the railing. "You must forgive me."

"Nonsense," Martha said. "It's only my new situation, Gandhi's sudden death, my husband's disappointment in me, and now poor Harilal's dying. I simply can't decide whether or not I'm doing the right thing, sailing around the world like this for no good reason. I should be back home with my family, growing older and sleepier in my own kitchen and wondering whom I can invite in for dinner. I should for once in my life have been sensible and satisfied with what I had," she said, "and not forever have gone panting after something more. And now, as my punishment, here I am, lost in the middle of an unknown ocean, almost at the end of a voyage that I'm sure won't be of much help to anyone."

After a moment, Dr. Rao tentatively proposed another interpretation. "It may be," he advised her, "that you need only to change your viewpoint a bit, see this adventure more as the beginning of something rather than the end, perhaps as the start of your own kind of *sannyasa*."

"Come again?"

"Tell me, Mrs. Houghton," he asked from behind a lecturer's raised hand, "you were at one time in your early life a student, yes?"

"Yes."

"And later, obviously, a housewife and a mother?"

Martha nodded at him, now becoming more interested.

"And now you and your husband are retired?"

"We are. But what are you getting at?" she asked him.

"Only that, in your own way, you've already passed through three of the four distinct *asramas,* or stages — four seasons, if you will — of a Hindu's life. I won't bore you with their names, but suffice it to say that the period now lying before you is the best and the holiest of them all. It is a time of going forth into homelessness, as free and lonely as a great swan, discovering the connection — the identity even — between your own soul and the great soul of the universe." He turned toward Martha, and she saw how kind and trustworthy his face appeared in the haze of the ship's running lights. "Only by visiting each of these hill stations along the line can a man — or a woman, too, yes — hope to make a whole, round life. My own father's *sannyasa* was a time of joy to him, as I pray mine shall be for me. He discarded all his possessions, even most of his clothing, took leave of his loved ones, and set out to walk the length and breadth of India with nothing but a *dhoti* around his waist and a begging bowl in his hands. We never heard from him again, but continue to hope that he fulfilled his solitary fate. Didn't our Gandhiji intend the same thing when he wrote that he wished someday to reduce himself to zero?"

Before Martha could object, the philosopher concluded, "No, no, but I see the same destiny lying in wait for you, my dear lady. Whatever may have brought you here is of no material consequence, do you understand? It doesn't matter," he exclaimed, "where you are going now or why. All that is important is that you go."

When the two finally parted, Martha went back to her cabin with a somewhat lighter step. Dr. Rao had, as Hetta had predicted, soothed some of her worst misgivings and given her something new and exciting to think about. By morning, when the earliest yellow stratum of the subcontinent began to make itself seen, it was Martha who was the first to pack, though there were still stockings and sleeves hanging messily outside her valise.

Bombay — India itself — was nothing at all what Martha had expected it to be. Instead of a mess of political disorder on the Mazagon Dock, she encountered only an intense and stimulating liveliness. Even now, after the peak of the warm season, the humid air seemed too heavy to breathe in, yet at the same time it bathed the throat and lungs with an incense-laden wash. On landfall, Dr. Rao had been kind enough to stand with her and the rest of the paying passengers and describe the city as it came into view — the human restlessness of Chowpatty Beach, the Queen's Necklace of apartment buildings and shops skirting along Back Bay, and the buff-colored basalt of the Afghan church near the tip of the Colaba peninsula. Once the *Ranchi* had made fast to the pilings in Bombay Harbor, the exchange of goods and people was accomplished in a matter of hours. Martha had gathered up the names and addresses of her traveling companions, wished the navigator good luck with his future career, and found herself in a rattling taxicab with the Indian professor before she knew what was happening. It was somehow decided that she would stay with him and his family for a few days until they could locate Harilal Gandhi, and she only had time to be grateful that back home she'd had the foresight to bring her newest nightgown.

The drive to Dr. Rao's home in the Parel district north of Crawford Market was a steady barrage of impressions. Sitting close to the open window, Martha felt strangely invigorated by this unfamiliar sense of being lost and overwhelmed. Rainbows of hanging saris flickered past her eyes. London-style buses bullied their way through the metropolitan traffic, listing as the ship had to the left from the weight of men clinging to their platforms. At every stop, street vendors would rush the taxi with concoctions of puffed rice, potatoes, onions, and chutney on plates of green leaves, a delectable dish that Martha finally had to try. Farther on, pink-turbaned ear cleaners waved their silver spoons and vials of oil at her with half-toothed grins, while bicyclists with long trays of tiffin carriers ricocheted off the sides of the vehicle. They reached the philosopher's home in less than an hour, yet, as far as Martha could tell, there hadn't been the slightest reduction in the level of energetic madness surrounding them.

"My wife and daughters will be overjoyed to meet you," Dr. Rao said as he eagerly handed his guest out onto the pavement and began haggling with the driver.

"But do they even know I'm coming?" worried Martha.

"It doesn't matter. Visitors are like the gods in Indian homes. Always welcome."

Mrs. Rao, compact and beringed with inherited gold, turned out to be not so very different from any of the women back in Hedge End. When she wasn't managing her children's education or the house's money and its religious practices, she was cleaning her china for special occasions — the family usually ate off banana leaves — and mending cushions, which, in her case, involved reweaving palmyra mats with her bare hands. After a single afternoon in the company of her and her two spirited daughters, Martha felt perfectly at home, as if she had found parts of Rebecca Pye and Alice and Nellie here in the unlikeliest of places. She was helped in this by another wire from Paul that had been waiting for her at the P and O offices, promising her that Samuel was getting on handsomely, though he had lately developed the peculiar habit of inviting Dr. Little over for tea and long, intricate talks on life, death, and India. He had also started attending church again every Sunday.

The next morning, once Martha had managed to stop swaying whenever she stood, Dr. Rao began ferrying her about in search of the hospital that Harilal Gandhi had never specifically named in any of his three letters. They rode in taxis and suffocating buses from the great complex of the Jamsetjee Jeejeebhoy Hospital and the adjacent Grant Medical College to the Gothic face and imposing iron staircases of the Gokuldas Tejpal Hospital in Carnac Road. After the major institutions had failed them, they turned to smaller clinics and sanatoria in every section of the city. Day followed futile day, until they both came close to losing hope. Finally, the philosopher recalled a colleague of his who had taken refuge in a newly built hospital in Dharavi with the unlikely name of Sion. But even here there was no patient registered as Harilal Gandhi.

"Could it be," suggested Martha as they stood frustrated outside its doors, "that he wants to remain anonymous? Even back home, tuberculosis is sometimes still regarded as a shameful ailment. It's silly, really, but there it is. Besides," she went on, "as you've said, he hasn't always been the pride of his family."

Dr. Rao hurried off and in a minute returned with a triumphant smile. "I believe, madam, that you may have hit upon it. Inside," he whispered dramatically, "is a man in the ward for infectious diseases who is identified only as Number 8. But, by careful questioning and one or two *annas* changing hands, I've been able to determine that his first name is indeed Harilal and that he bears some resemblance to one whom every Indian should recognize."

Martha insisted on going in alone, and she begged Dr. Rao to resume the life that her arrival had interrupted. He seemed heartbroken at the news.

"But surely we'll be seeing you again this evening," he pleaded. "Where else will you eat and sleep?"

Instead of imposing on the Raos any longer, Martha decided to try to find a room in the vicinity of the hospital and asked him to send her things along. Then she walked toward the entrance, bracing herself for what she thought would be the kind of extended deathwatch that, since the loss of baby Walter some forty years ago, she had hoped she would never have to repeat.

12

MARTHA FALTERED for a moment in the entrance hall, though it would have taken one who knew her well to notice. She moved on toward the reception area, though not without wondering at how elongated the hallway suddenly appeared, how bloated and disembodied the faces, and how hollow the most solid objects felt to the touch. She soon recovered enough to charm her way into the ward with a story about an old family retainer who had gone missing. But, for the rest of the day and for the weeks to come, there stayed with her this odd sense of the unreal, the impression that — as Dr. Rao and his fellow Indians were always maintaining — all the world around her was a dream.

Inside the clinic, Martha passed from bed to bed, trying to leave a kind look with every patient behind his mist of white mosquito netting. Most of the men were ashen with hunger, but then so were most of the people outside the hospital, either sleeping or walking in the streets. Not a medical expert, she couldn't tell the insidious cancer from the long-term kidney collapse or the wasting away of alcoholism. Yet Martha did eventually come across a few horrid examples of facial disfigurement that she guessed might have been caused by leprosy or something even more unmentionable. And to these men she only nodded as if to tell them that she, too, could hardly bear to think of what lay in store for them and how little could be done.

Number 8, by an accident of architecture, was set apart in his own recess, not far from a window overlooking a maidan of yellow acacias bordered by busy roads. Like the others, his bed also had a bare metal frame and a canopy hung with gauze. An enameled table with a single drawer stood beside it. All the usual clinical sensations were there — the acidic odors, the clang of tin, chipped, coarse surfaces — with an additional element that Martha could not at first distinguish. Then she stopped in the middle of the floor and listened. The sound she heard was the combined chant of the men's breathing and moaning, a continuous, muffled ululation of suffering that might have come from a church in prayer or from a rank of electrical generators.

Martha knew the man in the eighth bed by sight, even though she'd never seen so much as a photograph of him. But Gandhi's eldest son was now approximately the same age that Gandhi himself had been when Martha had last met him in Chichester, seventeen years ago. Harilal could almost have been mistaken for his father in his old age, as he lay asleep in a wrapping of sheets with only his shaved head and feet protruding. They both possessed the same spectral leanness, though the older man's had come from self-denial and the younger's from dissipation and disease. In sleep, Harilal shared his father's hard chin and mouth, but on him the ears spread less, the brow stood heavier, and the nose was not as pronounced. The man in the bed, thought Martha, must have always been adept at frowning, either in concentration or discouragement. Over the years, she had garnered from Gandhi's letters and conversations the gist of the son's story, and on the *Ranchi* Dr. Rao had filled in the remaining gaps. Generational distrust, a father experimenting with a son whom he had always for some reason resented, the boy kicking over the traces at an early age, followed by decades of two loves working at cross-purposes — all this she had been prepared for. But what now brought her to a halt was a vision of the end of that process, the dying of a man whose life he had never felt to be entirely his own.

Careful not to disturb anyone in the ward, Martha dragged a chair over to the bedside and began her vigil. She sat unmoving for more than an hour, ignoring the stares of the other patients and fending off the curiosity of the circulating nurses. When the afternoon sun fell low enough to stir the mosquito netting with its heat, some distant noise awakened the sleeper, and he saw his visitor. The frown that Martha had been expecting all along finally appeared.

"I've come," she said in answer to his look. "As you asked."

"I?"

Martha slipped out of her pocket a photograph that Samuel had never found in the house, a portrait of herself and Gandhi as young friends in Portsmouth.

"Are these the kinds of pictures of your father and me that you claim to have? And are the letters any more damning?"

Realization slowly came over the sick man as wind over water, rolling an expression of utter incredulity up into his forehead.

"You? Mrs." — he had to search for her name — "Mrs. Houghton? But this is impossible! I never dreamt for a moment that you would actually come."

"Yet here I am." Martha made a show of straightening her

sleeves and sniffing, as if her being in a hospital in Bombay was nothing extraordinary. But, privately, she was exulting over the effect that her long journey was having. "I only thought," she went on in a casual tone, "that, with your father having been taken from us both so abruptly, you might need someone of his age who knew him well to keep you company. Strength of mood, you know, is what's required to pull you through this trial. I only wish that my aunt Feemy had had as much in her struggle with the illness."

As weak as he was, Harilal started squirming uneasily beneath his bedclothes, perhaps hoping to scuttle away from the apparition before him. "Oh, dear lady," he pleaded with his hands raised between them, "how can you ever forgive me?"

"But I thought the need to be forgiven was what we had most in common," Martha reminded him gently. "That, and your father, of course. I suppose I came to see you as much for his sake as for yours. Ever since his death, I've been trying to sort out my feelings about him, what he was to me. But he was so many things to so many people around the world" — she shook her head — "that sometimes one forgets that he was also just a man with friends, a wife, sons. It takes away something important from his memory, don't you think, when everyone does that, especially those of us who knew him personally?"

Harilal's eyes swung from side to side. "And your husband?" he asked in a low voice. "Did he accompany you here?"

"No," Martha answered shortly. "Samuel doesn't see these things in the same way that I do."

"Ah, the revelations!" Seeing her start, he explained, "Your name, your story in the English press, reached us some time ago. I was so sorry to read all the lies and exaggerations. It must have been very hurtful for you both."

"Well, most of that has quieted down. And it was never so bad, even at its worst."

"Was it that that separated you from your husband?" the man in the bed inquired after a moment's thought. "I hope it wasn't my letters to you!"

"No, no, don't fluster yourself so."

Harilal tried to sit up, propping his body on his elbows and baring his sunken chest. The wings of his shoulders stood out in agonizing relief, and a cough bubbled and wheezed at the top of his throat.

"Lie back down," Martha commanded professionally, and she tucked the sheets under his withered haunches. "I didn't come here to upset you. If you're to get well, you must mind your doctors and nurses and all of us who only want the best for you. What about your family? Do you have any relatives here in Bombay or near enough to be called in?"

"My brother, Devadas . . . my son, Kanti." He waved the topic aside as if he were too ashamed to talk about those whom he had hurt so often.

Martha turned the conversation toward safer ground. She told him about her adventures en route to India, about her tour of Mediterranean seaports, their delay in the Suez Canal, and the kindness of Dr. Rao, whose name Harilal pretended to recognize. Within an hour, the two were almost at perfect ease with each other. The sick man appreciated the attention and even glared at his neighbors in the ward to challenge them to match such a notable guest. Now that the British were officially out of the country, the once hated rulers had become for some coveted acquisitions, like the headless or noseless statues of Queen Victoria and Lord Sandhurst that graced many Indian gardens. Harilal couldn't help beaming in pride at the Western-dressed, fair-skinned lady who had come to give solace to him and him alone. The nature of Martha's reaction, however, was far more complicated.

To say that she saw her old friend in his eldest son was altogether too simple. She seemed to see more of him in Harilal than she had ever seen in Gandhi himself when he was alive. This realization confused her and bent her closer to the bed as though for a clearer view. She had, over the span of forty years, met Gandhi face to face only during his five trips to England, and all those meetings had been in loud restaurants, hostels, railway stations, hotel lobbies, and on cautious walks. Seldom had they ever been truly alone, and even then his thoughts were usually elsewhere or he'd had to run off to some conference or appointment. Their friendship had played itself out mainly by letter, cable, and telephone, voices without expressions that were forced to be abbreviated and condensed beyond all human dimensions. It had often put Martha in mind of the classical Chinese that Rebecca, who knew a little, sometimes translated for her, where a handful of words — "no inside no outside" — could contain an entire philosophy. Yet Martha and Gandhi had finally become very skilled at the exercise. Their letters and discussions had never been long-winded, but terse, epigrammatic shorthand that, like poetry, spoke volumes in a few lines. In this way, as their relationship had grown, they'd become something of a couple, supplementing their briefest remarks with a background of common associations. It had all been quite satisfying, though forever tinged with the loneliness of two people who had never completely learned each other's language.

But now, here today with Harilal, Martha was being offered the chance to spend as much time as she wanted with one of the Gandhi men, and she intended to revel in every moment. As she continued to look at the figure in the bed and saw him look back at her, she suddenly broke a short silence by beginning, "Do you know, Mr. Gandhi —"

"Harilal, please, madam."

"Harilal." She smiled at him in gratitude. "I was going to say that I can see so much of your father in you, in your eyes and in the tilt of your head, in your profile. It's a marvel!"

He seemed offended by the comparison. "A pity he never thought so."

"Oh, I'm sure he did. You shouldn't say such things. Sons always fight with their fathers, and vice versa. It never really means as much as they think it does at the time." Martha absently patted the counterpane and added, "I know my own son, Paul, has had plenty of problems with his father. They've always viewed everything in life so differently. They've fought and made up, moped and roared with laughter, and shared some sort of masculine code that still drives the girls and me mad. But even after the worst of it, they're still close, only in their own way. I imagine it's hard not to be, when every morning Paul has to stand before his shaving mirror and see his father's face staring back at him."

"But has your son, this Paul, ever lied to your husband?" Harilal grumbled.

"I suppose he has, yes. Most of us do, don't we, at one time or another?"

"And has he ever cheated him," Harilal persisted, "and misrepresented and humiliated him and sent long, awful letters about him to all his friends and associates? And has he been such a bitter disappointment to his father, tell me, that his father has had to disown him in the press by warning everyone that 'men may be good, not necessarily their children'? And," he added, as he gazed blindly at the sheets he was twisting in his hands, "were both his wife and he left to die alone because their firstborn son was too drunk to stand beside them in their hour of greatest need? To this day, I swear to you, I don't even remember mourning them."

Alarmed by his distress, and expecting any minute to be ushered out of the ward for the night, Martha repeated her previous consolations and promised Harilal that she would come every day for as long as it took him to get better.

"But you must buck up," she ordered him as she reached for her handbag, "and put some more meat on your bones. Right now, you look as if you, too, were trying to reduce yourself to zero."

"I rather like your way of saying that," Harilal muttered bleakly.

"You should. It's your father's."

She left him to rest and made her way to the nearest lodging *chawl,* where, for a small fee, she was given a rolled mattress and a wooden frame at the end of what amounted to a hallway in a private home. From there, Martha returned to Sion Hospital every day for the next two weeks or so, finally establishing a schedule that was as comforting to her as it was to her patient. Every morning, she would have tea and biscuits with him and try to get him to take a bit of fish from the Koli woman in the skintight sari who serviced the area. Then they would talk or sit silent or thumb through English and Indian newspapers together, commenting on the state of the world and the latest merchandise. At lunch, Martha would leave him alone with his doctors and go out for a walk in the streets around the hospital, wondering when exactly Samuel would telegraph her as a sign that he'd finally acknowledged — as her daughters had at tea with her in Portsmouth — her own separate needs. The seasonal rains were coming closer and closer, and broad clouds hung like drops of indigo ink above palm trees tousled by winds off the Arabian Sea. The heat clung to her face, but it also drew out from the vegetation puffs of blossoms, leaves longer than her arm, and exposed tubers that oozed moisture. Even the littered children who lived and slept in the roadway developed a patina on their colorful rags so that, in the right light, they shone as if bathed in pastel dyes. Rabid dogs hopped about in expectation of water, while birds that no one could name united the trees with swathes of motion. By the time Martha got back to the ward, Harilal would be ready for their daily card games and an afternoon tea of mangoes and unleavened *puris,* after which he would lie back on his pillow and chew betel with his gray gums and she would nap in her chair. Harilal's condition always worsened at night, and then Martha politely retreated. Nevertheless, she always felt as if she carried the dampness of his cough back to her room in her clothes.

The patient had, it appeared, other visitors as well. Packets of sweets would mysteriously sprout on his bedside table, along with extinguished cigarettes, sums of cash, and once a forgotten set of keys. With the habitual delicacy of the outsider, Martha never asked whose these were, and Harilal never gave an explanation. Family, no doubt, and perhaps old friends were gathering around to lend their support, and in such a situation Martha had to feel something like an interloper. Her relationship with Harilal was nascent, indirect, more of an offshoot or a graft than a thing with roots. As eager as she was to help, she knew her limits and was careful not to presume too much on too slender a connection. Yet she would never have come so far if she hadn't had a good reason for doing so, and now she believed that she had a kind of solace that no one else could have to offer her old friend's unhappy son.

To offer herself, too. The next time she saw Harilal, she asked him, "How was it you first came to find out about me anyway? From your father's papers or my letters? Or did he ever happen to mention my name?"

"Not really, no. But then he didn't have to."

"I'm not sure what you mean."

"Mrs. Houghton," Harilal clarified, still refusing to call her Martha even in private, "it may have been because I was the firstborn that I was the most sensitive. To my father's moods, that is. I could tell his every thought and feeling simply by the way he entered a room. Whether he was content or distracted or, yes, even angry, I could see it in the way he held his head and moved his limbs. Truly," Harilal mused, his cheeks flushed, "I do believe it's my first recollection of him, how he stood before me once after I'd struck one of my younger brothers and didn't move, didn't speak, only stared at me as if I were lost to him forever.

"But later," he went on after a pause, "when I grew old enough to understand him more, I was able to interpret such signals better, not only about myself, but about others, too. And then, I think, was when I began to wonder if part of his heart weren't far, far away from his home here in India."

"Of course, he had so many varied interests abroad," she observed in an effort to lead him further on, "here and in South Africa and Europe, that it must have been difficult for anyone to know where his thoughts were tending. There's no reason why I should have been singled out."

"Do you recall his Lancashire visit?" Harilal asked her.

"To the women of the cotton mills? In 'thirty-one? Yes, I've seen some of the photographs."

"Well, my mother, bless her, used to tease him on his return from that final journey to England, telling him that she wasn't sure she could trust him with all those beautiful foreign ladies who were constantly surrounding him. She did trust him," Harilal hastened to assure her, "and besides, as you probably know, my parents hadn't been that way with each other for over twenty-five years."

"Your father told me as much once," Martha whispered delicately, "in a letter."

"My mother, I don't think, ever felt the lack too sorely," Harilal declared with a certain prim devotion. "Women never do. And even in him the vow of *brahmacharya,* of chastity in marriage, cleansed him somehow and made his work more effective. Everyone admired him terribly for it, both Indians and Westerners. But I," he faltered, "I always asked myself what that must have done to his love for my mother. Because I could never imagine any love, either between a man and a woman or between a father and a son, that didn't have some touching in it."

His thoughts wandered, as the daily fever of his illness seemed to fight his urge to make himself understood. Martha was thankful that, because of his worldwide travels, Harilal's English was noticeably clearer than Dr. Rao's. So now, to help him along, she merely had to murmur the word "love" a few times for him to pick up the thread again.

"Yes, that was when I first suspected that he might have — someone else. He used to tell us, oh, how many times a day, 'If you can't love England, at least love the English. For there must be,' he'd say, 'over there as here, so many honest men and women who are no different from us and who wish us no harm.' Then he would go on to describe that typical housewife in York or Liverpool or Bath, I don't know where." Harilal flailed his arms above his head. "But it never seemed to occur to anyone — anyone but me — that he might have had a single, actual woman in mind, that he must have had one to make her sound so personal and real."

"Are you trying to say —"

"You were his ideal, madam, his standard!" Harilal said

with a tired smile. "I'm certain of it. You were the one he was thinking of whenever he spoke about the goodness in the hearts of our masters. He'd tell us again and again, even us children, that our only hope lay in the common folk, in all the peasants and workers and householders who kept the engines of the different nations running. And, among all these," he finished, "my father praised most the simple wives and mothers — like my own, like you — who never failed in their daily duties. These, he said, were the true great souls of this world, not himself."

"I should have thought," Martha said as an aside, "that, as close as you always were to your mother, you'd still be angry with me for stealing so much of your father's affections away from her."

"Oh, I was, Mrs. Houghton, for years and years. But now who has the time?" Harilal almost laughed, then closed his eyes and exhaled. "I've spent so many, many years simply being angry with myself."

Martha withdrew as soon as she saw that their conversation was weakening him. Yet, as she walked back to the boarding house through the earliest hint of June's coming downpour, she chafed at how much she still wanted to learn from Harilal and how little time was left. There were still so many things that she didn't understand about Gandhi — about his daily habits and his nighttime dreams and the way he laughed with children — all those minor, secret insights that only a legal wife can know. Martha continued to turn the matter compulsively over in her head, as she fell asleep to the sound of prayers being chanted next door and the rusted-metal smell of descending rain outside.

On the next day, the monsoon began in earnest. Great volumes of water fell from the sky as if over a cliff. Drumbeats bounced off the streets up to the height of a man, and winds made whole neighborhoods of shacks lean in one direction. Martha tried half a dozen times to brave the two or three blocks to the hospital, but each of her efforts was beaten back by swells that drenched her even under an awning. She tried to hail a taxi, only to watch the drivers wave their palms before their faces in resignation. Umbrellas were of little use. They collapsed like wet drake wings and blinded their users so badly that they toddled into ditches. The locals who stood with her at the door seemed to welcome their imprisonment. They traded *bidis* back and forth, grinned down at their open shirts, and filled their chests with the refreshing humidity. Martha shook her head over their childish nonchalance, but then she remembered that now, because of her departed friend, they were finally free. Free to err, granted, as well as to succeed, but free to take either course entirely on their own. As, she supposed, was she.

At midafternoon, when the storm eased off enough for birds to fly again, Dr. Rao suddenly appeared in the rear of a rented car. He came up to Martha with a bedraggled envelope that he bore in his joined hands as though it were an order from an impatient raja. It was a telegram, still not from Samuel, but from "Paul, Nellie, Alice, Tetty, and Malcolm" and consisted of only two fragments: "ALL FORGIVEN STOP PLEASE COME HOME."

"When did this arrive?" she asked the professor.

"Today, I promise you. No more than an hour ago. Is there an answer?"

He tried to see past Martha's shoulder, perhaps to judge how these accommodations compared to his, but too many of the boarders had crowded into the front hallway.

"No. Well, not yet, at any rate." Martha pocketed the slip of paper and regarded Dr. Rao. "But would you mind horribly," she said, taking his arm, "having your man drive me over to the Sion? I'll buy you a tea for your trouble."

In the hospital's whitewashed cafeteria, Dr. Rao did his best to convince Martha that her mission would be to no avail, that she was only endangering her own health and the equanimity of her family back in England by staying on here any longer. The rains would bring frightful diseases, he told her, frightful, and Harilal Gandhi would die, and then where would she be? But Martha countered all his arguments with a peaceful nod, and when he'd gone she returned to the ward with a covered cup of broth for the man in bed Number 8.

Today Harilal Gandhi looked much better, as if he'd been scrubbed and rinsed from the wash of the rain against his window. His brow was drier and clear, and his more erect posture in the bed made him seem taller. Martha had been planning to question him further about her place in his father's thoughts, but when she sat down before him she found herself asking about his place instead.

"I know, I know," Martha said with the air of an aunt. "You say that your relationship with him was always strained and that he never understood or even cared for you. But do you really think now that was true?"

"Well —"

"You see, I know a bit more about your history than you might expect. Some your father told me, some I read in newspaper accounts, and some I've only learned since leaving England. Still, I've perhaps heard the worst," she assured him. "I already know of your frustration at his not allowing you to be properly educated. And I know that he forced you to submit to being jailed for his cause in South Africa and so kept you from your wife and children. And I know of your unsatisfying work as a commercial traveler and all the losses and mistakes since then. Not to mention how much you must have blamed him for your mother's death and even, in some ways, for her life.

"But all these are in the past now, far, far in the past." Martha tipped her chair toward the head of the bed and reached out for Harilal's hand. "What I want to know is how you feel today," she pleaded with him, "about your father, about me, about everything. If we're going to bring you through this crisis — and we will! — then you must come to some sort of peace with all that's happened."

During this, their final conversation, Martha and Harilal came as near as they ever would to some degree of fellowship. Whether it was because Martha was almost the same age that his mother had been at her death, or because they both felt the need to hurry, they were soon talking more frankly than either of them had in years. Harilal puzzled over the unevenness of his past, raged at his father, blamed him, then blamed himself, and at last lay back exhausted by the sheer incomprehensibility of life. For her part, Martha reviewed her long marriage and her even longer relationship with Gandhi, and she couldn't help but see them as two halves of the same whole. In the end, she and the sick man reached not a single profound conclusion about love or forgiveness, until they decided that perhaps their very ignorance might have been the most profound conclusion possible. To make their friendship eternal, the Indian sprinkled some of his lunch salt in a glass of water and showed Martha how to do the same.

At the end of the afternoon, they pored together over a copy of the *Bhagavad Gita*, both Harilal's and his father's constant companion, and he translated one of his favorite passages for Martha. "'What of the man who strives and fails and yet has faith, O Krishna?'" he read. "'What becomes of him?'" The answer seemed to give him some measure of hope: "'Neither in this world nor in the world to come shall this man ever pass away.'"

But then he closed the volume with a downcast look. "That was the one area, I suppose, where I disappointed my father the most," he admitted. "In my never being quite perfect enough for him."

"Yet I always considered that to be *his* greatest imperfection," Martha said in some surprise. "That maddening, inhuman perfection of his that always got in the way of his loving."

On the nineteenth of June, a Saturday, Martha was delayed slightly on her way to Sion Hospital by rising late and by the continuing rains. Making her way down the street, she suddenly decided that today she would send a wire to Samuel as soon as she was done seeing to Harilal. This stubborn pride of both husband and wife had been allowed to go on long enough. Waiting for the other to reach out first was as pointless as waiting for the monsoon to stop, which it always did, but in its own good time. Besides, Martha didn't really need any more contact from Hedge End for her to realize what Samuel was going through. After all their years together, she knew that his hurt and his anger would eventually give way to denial, then to understanding, and finally to an acceptance that was so much greater than mere forgiveness because it would have no condescension in it. This was how it had always worked between them because, like a pair of twins, they usually thought each other's thoughts and felt each other's feelings at the same time.

When Martha reached the ward, she saw that Number 8 was empty, and she stood still in disbelief. A passing nurse informed her that all had been taken care of by the dead man's family and that she need concern herself no longer. Nothing had been left behind, except a packet of old, yellowed letters and faded photographs, neatly wrapped and consigned to "Mrs. Houghton." She didn't know what to do with herself, but, since it was still early and the rain was bearing down outside, she began to make the rounds of the other beds to see how she might help the remaining patients. That night, Martha didn't get back home until well past ten o'clock.

13

TEMPORARILY SET ADRIFT by Harilal Gandhi's death, Martha telegraphed Samuel that she would be home as soon as she'd finished the Perth leg of her voyage. She still owed her brother both for the ticket and for a long overdue visit, and she said she could use the time to come to terms with all her recent losses. She also had to fulfill a shipboard promise to Dr. Rao to accompany him to the Hindu caves on Elephanta Island. Only then would she be perfectly free to return.

"The others from the *Ranchi* have already gone, I'm afraid so, to their various destinations," Dr. Rao said regretfully as he oversaw his wife's preparation of their picnic lunch of *chapattis*, green beans, lentil soup, and yogurt. She slapped his hands away, for she made the same meal every day for the neighborhood *dabbawallah* to bicycle to him at his university office. "But there is no reason why we shouldn't still enjoy ourselves immensely. You can see," he added with a wave out the one window, "that I have chosen perfect weather, or nearly so. And, if we can only leave within the next five minutes, we should be on the island and sightseeing to our hearts' content by noon."

Half an hour later, Martha and the philosopher and his two daughters were on their way, Mrs. Rao having never trusted any travel over water. The day was hardly fine, though somewhat more bearable than usual. The clouds were higher in the sky and lighter, and the wet air had in it an unidentifiable tinge of sweetness. They reached the harbor in good time and boarded the island ferry with a tide of German and Cambodian tourists who hadn't been fazed in the slightest by the country's recent political changes. The ship set out with a sag into a trough that almost confirmed Mrs. Rao's superstitions, but then it righted itself and turned its nose stoutly into the waves.

The rest of the hourlong ride across the bay was uneventful. Martha sat apart from her companions and surveyed the high-prowed fishing sailboats, some of which were tending nets, while others were making for the open sea. The Raos conversed in Gujarati behind her, agreeing that Mrs. Houghton had aged visibly in the last weeks, the former spring in her posture and her ruddy complexion now almost entirely gone. The death of her friend in Sion Hospital had physically collapsed her into a smaller, diaphanous version of herself. Something precious and strong seemed to have left her for good, and now she sat stooped and spoke rarely, as if she could no longer do battle against either life or death.

As soon as the island rose like a tree-crowned barrow on the horizon, Dr. Rao took charge of his party and fashioned a *pagri* for each of them, so that the thin muslin scarves should hang down from their sun helmets and protect their necks.

"Without the rains," he observed as he shepherded them

toward the railing, "the sky shall be on fire throughout the day and, especially after the cool darkness of the caves, will bear down upon us. We surely don't want our friend's last memory of India to be one of sunstroke and prostration. And," he finished pedantically, "there are also vermin to be considered."

In a pouting daze, Martha let herself be guided toward the principal north entrance of the temple, her swollen ankles wobbling on the broken stones of the long stairs. Dr. Rao pointed out the first two figures flanking the doorway, Siva as Lakulisha and Siva as Nataraja. In the kind of exaggerated voice that people usually use in sickrooms, he lectured on and on about these two manifestations of his god, how they embodied the inward and outward aspects of the holy energy. His words carried through the main, low-ceilinged hollow of the cave, impressing even those visitors who understood no English. He and his daughters gestured ecstatically at the recessed images of Siva spearing the demon, Andhaka, and sitting with his consort, Parvati, in their mountain home of Kailasa. Even though the Raos had seen all this countless times before, they could barely contain their enthusiasm as they tried to inspire their guest with the site's contours, shadows, and divine expressions. But, as vigorously as she nodded at everything around her, Martha saw only cold rock and blackness and the faithful art of believers who were gone forever.

Then Dr. Rao steered them all directly toward the great triple-headed Trimurti that dominated the south wall. Confident that this figure, at least, would lift Mrs. Houghton out of her depths, he demonstrated how the tan-colored sculpture seemed to grow out of the living rock and how the profiles of the other two heads over the shoulders created a serene, androgynous trinity. His daughters mimicked their father's excitement, yet Martha continued to lag behind. She looked and shivered and mumbled a halfhearted appreciation that was absorbed at once by the impassive cave walls. All she could think of was how she had failed to be with Harilal when he died, as she had earlier failed to be with Gandhi during his final hour.

On an outcropping of rock that overlooked the harbor below, the four of them spread out their picnic handkerchiefs on a natural landing and made themselves comfortable. With food and tea from a thermos that reminded her of Samuel's, Martha began to feel more like herself again. She swept the hair back from her forehead, straightened her spine, and ate almost as much as the two girls combined. Dr. Rao claimed that it was all the doing of the local god, and no one in his company dared to contradict him.

"There is still some time before our scheduled return to the city," he pointed out as he stood and wiped his hands on a tuft of grass. "What do you say we look about the rest of the island? Girls? Mrs. Houghton? Are we all — how do you say it? — game?"

First, they explored the adjacent courts that flanked the main shrine, taking advantage of the relative lack of crowds on the perimeter. The two daughters supported Martha as if they were a pair of crutches, and the trio scrabbled after their leader with only the occasional whine and shortness of breath. After the temple complex itself, Dr. Rao wanted to mount the hill opposite the caves, from where, he vowed, the view of Bombay was never to be forgotten. To this suggestion, however, Martha finally had to object, begging off because of the suffocating heat and the questionable state of her joints. But she entreated the others to go on without her, and nothing any of the Raos could say would change her mind. She'd be waiting for them, she said, just inside the doorway, where she remembered there was a pocket of cool air and a ledge to sit on.

They escorted her back to the entrance and promised to return in less than an hour. "If you should want for anything," Dr. Rao told her, "anything at all, you have only to step out between these stone *dvarapalas* and shout my name. Do you think, madam, that you could cry 'Rasipuram Krishnaswami' loudly enough for us to hear?"

Martha said she could and, after they had gone, sought refuge from the seething afternoon light in the western sanctuary whose courtyard led to one cul-de-sac straight ahead and another off to the right. She walked into the former at once, mainly to escape the notice of the other tourists and to steady her spinning head. Here all was ice and dark, a smooth shell of mountain with the mineral touch that lies deep inside the body of the earth. A plume of condensation preceded her, and the ring of her shoes on the rock floor welcomed her in with a chorus of voices. The hollow had little to show for itself but two fluted columns and a cistern in which stagnant water puckered, drop by drop. What the purpose of this dead end had been some fourteen centuries earlier Martha could not see, unless it had been used as a shelter for those disciples who couldn't bear the direct gaze of the resident god. In any event, today it was quiet and lonely enough even for her, and she paced around its complete circuit twice as though she were in a trance.

After a while, she wandered out of the semicircular alcove and moved toward the smaller niche. This one was more shallow, a natural cavity that in the beginning might have needed only a minimal digging out. The reflected glare of daylight gave it a silent, brooding aspect, but such solitude she now cherished. The bustle of the Germans and the Cambodians receded into the confined bowels of the temple, outside the drone of insects and grasses sounded as restful as snoring, and beyond that the massive wash of the harbor seemed to cut the island off from all modern life. Time did not stand still exactly, but it did take on a sluggish, viscid quality that slowed and dulled her as if she'd just dragged her feet through tar or birdlime.

Gingerly, Martha stepped inside the recess, but found nothing. Darkness engulfed her, and the lingering choke of incense almost drove her away. Then, after a few moments, she was able to distinguish the shape of the relief sculpture on her right. As with most of the works on Elephanta Island, the figure had been coaxed out of the stone wall and made to stand as one of the jutting bones of the mountain itself. Later Martha would be informed that it was a representation of Siva as the Lord of Yogis, as Yogishvara. But to her at first, except for the typical ornate Hindu headdress, the seated man reminded her of the Buddha in a similar pose. The statue was only partial now, its arms having broken off and its lap regressed into messy shards. Yet the upper torso and the head were intact, and the absolute tranquillity of the god shone out of the rock face. She studied the yogi and his surrounding attendants for a long while, transfixed by their total timelessness, until she finally turned toward the opposite display.

This one was far more animated. Here the god was dancing, each of his four arms counterbalancing his turned hips and the stylized movements of his truncated legs. One of his left hands appeared to be lifting a veil, which Dr. Rao had already identified as the veil of the world's illusion. Siva's crowned head was tilted a few degrees to one side, listening to inaudible music perhaps or simply dreaming. To his right, the cave wall was thronging with miniatures, of himself sitting cross-legged, of serpents and rods and human beings at different stages of escape from the stone's embrace. The effect was of the physical planet itself coming alive with forms in motion. Once, Martha recalled, during an early meeting between them, Gandhi had suggested a radical notion. "What if we've been mistaken all this time?" he'd asked her. "What if everything we see — trees and stars and pebbles and light and the wind across the water, everything! — what if it really *is* all alive and conscious? How much reverence shall we have to show when we discover that even the fabrics of our very clothes have souls?" Now, as Martha continued to stare at the frozen dance before her and thought of his words, all of the many characters in the sculpture began to move.

It was only a trick of the light, of course, or the result of looking at one thing for too long without blinking. She knew that. Yet, at the same time, the shadows of the god and his companions did shift palpably in rhythmic, spasmodic motions. First they leaned nearer, then reared back, like a fluttering film at a cinema. Then they oscillated from side to side against each other, ticktocking in a way that made her feel dizzy. Finally, the whole tableau heaved and pirouetted and turned its faces into and out of the mountain as if they were being rapidly born and reborn. Martha's eyes started to water, and she found that she couldn't budge. The carvings that had been left behind by artists long since dead seemed to move in a kind of harmony, one not unlike the balanced bass and soprano tones that her church choir achieved on its best evenings. A song celestial . . .

With the fall of the sun toward Bombay, the light in the air became uncertain, painting shadows that lengthened and multiplied. Before long, their numbers exceeded those of the tourists themselves as the ferries pushed off with their final loads. The last glimpse that Martha and the Raos had of the island was as a half-submerged statue, turning its back on the harbor for the night.

Less than a week later, on the Mazagon Dock, Martha walked up to the first purser she saw and asked him which of the two waiting ships was bound for Perth.

"The one on the left, madam," he informed her. "Fremantle, actually. But Perth is right next door to it."

"And the other one?"

"Back home. And don't I wish I were on it!"

They ambled aimlessly together down the quay as they talked, while street boys and gulls converged near them. Since her visit to Elephanta Island, Martha had begun to get her energy back, yet she was still undecided about which course she ought to take, straight home or on toward new sights and new sounds.

"Tell me," she said to the purser. "What sort of passengers do you have on your Australian route?"

"Mostly emigrants, this time from Scotland. The shipping companies are still trying to make up for all the revenues and years they lost to the war. Mass transports like ours are their best option for now."

"No religious pilgrims going forth into homelessness?" Martha inquired. "I've heard that sometimes they travel by such means."

"This voyage, no. But, on the last circuit, we did carry a number of them from here to Ceylon. They made more than a sight on deck," he declared, "with all their naked, hungry bellies and their sacred threads and whatnot. They gave us rather a festive air."

When they came to a bend in the quay, Martha wondered aloud if her ticket for Perth could be used for either ship. She could always, she thought, make it up to Philip somehow.

"I don't see why not," the purser answered. "There's always room for paying guests, and at this time of the season you shouldn't even have to give them much notice. And, seeing as they'll both be pushing off at about the same time, you won't even have to decide until the last minute. Do you think that should satisfy?"

"Perfectly," Martha nodded, thanked him, and strolled off alone. On her way, she took out of her handbag the wire from Samuel that she'd received just this morning and read it over once again: ALL MOTOR JOURNALS BURNED STOP SHED TORN DOWN STOP NOW REBUILDING US STOP S. The old ironmonger, she reflected, still had his own rough way with words.

Then Martha came to a halt and for the longest time contemplated the pair of opposing ships. On a round planet, going home and not going home were eventually one and the same thing. Even when the last two whistles blew, she still hadn't chosen, though the monsoon winds at her back appeared to be leaning her more toward one than the other.